MW00759620

Native Americans: The Struggle for the Plains

GLOBE BOOK COMPANY
A Division of Simon & Schuster
Englewood Cliffs, New Jersey

Consultants:
Dr. David Beaulieu
Commissioner of Human Rights for the State of Minnesota
St. Paul, Minnesota

Jeffrey Hamley
Director of the Harvard Native American Program
Harvard University, Cambridge, Massachusetts

Executive Editor: Stephen Lewin
Editorial Consultant: Deborah A. Parks
Project Editor: Dan Zinkus
Assistant Editor: Kirsten Richert
Art Director: Nancy Sharkey
Designer: Armando Baez
Production Manager: Winston Sukhnanand
Marketing Manager: Elmer Ildefonso
Book Design: Keithley & Associates
Maps and Diagrams: Function Thru Form Inc.
Electronic Page Production: Function Thru Form Inc.
Photo Research: Omni-Photo Communications, Inc.

Photo Acknowledgments:
7: National Museum of American Art, Washington, D.C./Art Resource,
NY. 13: Coffrens Old West Gallery. 23: The Granger Collection. 25, 32:
Western History Collections, University of Oklahoma Library. 35, 36, 41,
51: The Granger Collection. 53, 55, 64: Bettmann Archive. 67: Montana
Historical Society, Helena. 68: Smithsonian Institute, Washington, D.C.
72: National Park Service, Nez Perce National Historical Park, Dr. Gor-
don and Rowena Alcorn Collection. 78: Historical Pictures, Chicago. 80:
Western History Collection, University of Oklahoma Library. 82: Michi-
gan and Family History Department, Grand Rapids Public Library. 85:
Smithsonian Institute, Washington, D. C.

Cover: Plains Native Americans setting out on a buffalo hunt in the
1800s. (Bettmann Archive)

ISBN: 0-835-90489-X

Printed in the United States of America 1 2 3 4 5 6 7 8 9 10 97 96 95 94 93 92

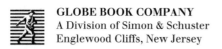
GLOBE BOOK COMPANY
A Division of Simon & Schuster
Englewood Cliffs, New Jersey

CONTENTS

SPIRIT OF THE PLAINS

THINKING ABOUT THE CHAPTER

What ways of life developed among Native Americans who settled on the Great Plains?

I n the month called "the Moon of the Popping Trees" (December), in the year of "the Winter When the Four Crows Were Killed" (1863), a Lakota Sioux woman named White Cow Sees gave birth to a child. The infant boy was given the name Black Elk — the same name given to his father, grandfather, and great-grandfather. Black Elk grew up listening to the stories of the "long-hairs," or older members of his people. The long-hairs helped preserve the history of the Lakota. "A people without history," a Lakota saying goes, "is like wind on the buffalo grass." Like a gust of wind, a people might soon disappear if they forgot their history.

At age 9, Black Elk had an amazing vision. In it, a group of long-hairs spoke to him. The long-hairs took Black Elk on a spectacular mystical journey that revealed the sacred ways of the Lakota.

Yet, as the 1900s opened, Black Elk feared that Lakota ways might be lost forever. He had lived to see settlers push the Lakota off their homelands on the northern Great Plains onto a strip of land in Pine Ridge, South Dakota. Soon the long-hairs who remem-

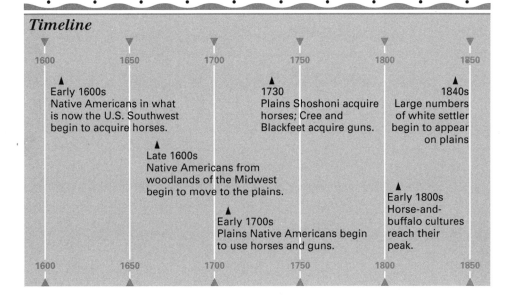

Timeline

1600	1650	1700	1750	1800	1850

Early 1600s
Native Americans in what is now the U.S. Southwest begin to acquire horses.

Late 1600s
Native Americans from woodlands of the Midwest begin to move to the plains.

Early 1700s
Plains Native Americans begin to use horses and guns.

1730
Plains Shoshoni acquire horses; Cree and Blackfeet acquire guns.

1840s
Large numbers of white settler begin to appear on plains

Early 1800s
Horse-and-buffalo cultures reach their peak.

bered the traditional ways of the people would be dead. Would the spirit of the Lakota then disappear like "wind on the buffalo grass"?

This chapter describes the Great Plains when the region was populated almost exclusively by Native Americans such as the Lakota. In Black Elk's words: "It is a story of all life that is . . . good to tell, and of us two-leggeds sharing in it with the four-leggeds." The rest of the chapters in this book trace the forces that shattered the world into which Black Elk and others of his generation were born.

1 BUFFALO PEOPLE AND HORSE NATIONS

How did Native Americans make use of the land and animals of the Great Plains?

The Lakota and other Native Americans on the Great Plains felt strong ties to the earth and all of earth's creatures. Bonds with nature led Native Americans to see the Great Plains differently than the settlers who would one day take the land from them. Explained Chief Luther Standing Bear of the Oglala band of the Lakota:

We did not think of the great open plains, the beautiful rolling hills, and winding streams with tangled growth, as *wild* . . . . To us it was tame. Earth was bountiful and we were surrounded with . . . blessings.

The Rhythm of the Seasons The settlers from the east, who began coming onto the plains in large numbers in the 1840s, saw the region as a grass-filled wilderness. Here and there, groves of willows and cottonwoods sprouted up along the banks of rivers and streams. But for the most part, sweeping fields of grass, called **prairies**, stretched as far as the eye could see. In the east, where rain fell heaviest, the grass grew tall and thick. In the west, where less rain fell, the grass grew shorter. This short grass proved ideal for the huge herds of white-tailed antelope and shaggy buffalo that roamed the plains. So many buffalo grazed on the short-bladed grass that it became known as buffalo grass.

The climate of the plains was harsh. In summer, a hot sun blazed down and parched much of the land. In the winter, frigid winds whipped out of the Rockies and covered the central and northern plains with snow.

Native Americans, however, had learned to live with the rhythm of the seasons. From spring to autumn, most groups followed the herds of grass-eating animals. When snow flurries filled the air, they moved to winter camps along the edges of the plains or in sheltered river valleys. This rhythm of life led Native Americans, such as the Lakota, to measure time by the cycles of the moon and to count their years in terms of memorable events in winter.

The Thunder of Hooves The animal that dominated life on the plains was the buffalo. A buffalo measured up to six feet (2 meters) from hoof to shoulder and weighed up to 2,000 pounds (900 kilograms). Experts have estimated that there were about 60 to 100 million buffalo in the mid-1800s. Their shaggy coats sometimes darkened the landscape for miles. Their thundering hooves shook the earth.

The huge buffalo herds made it possible for Native Americans to live on the plains. The buffalo supplied Native Americans with most of their needs: flesh for food, skins for shelter and clothing, bones for tools and weapons.

A family wrapped an infant in soft buffalo skins at birth and buried loved ones in buffalo robes at death. To honor the buffalo, many parents used the word *cow* in their daughters' names and *bull* in their sons'. Many hunters thanked a slain buffalo by placing its heart on the ground so that the buffalo's spirit might return to the herd.

In the 1830's, Native Americans still hunted buffalo by disguising themselves in wolf skins, as this painting by artist George Catlin illustrates.

Until the mid-1700s, most Native Americans on the plains hunted the buffalo on foot. They clad themselves in the skins of wolves or buffalo calves and crept up on the herds. The nearsighted buffalo rarely were aware of the Native Americans until the hunters stood to drive lances into their sides. But such a hunt required great courage. A wounded buffalo might stampede an entire herd or trample the hunters. Native Americans preferred, when possible, to drive the buffalo over cliffs.

New Arrivals—Two-Legged and Four-Legged In the late 1600s and early 1700s, new groups of Native Americans from the east appeared on the plains. These newcomers were seeking to escape the pressures of white settlement in the east and also to share in the rich resources of the plains. Native Americans spilled across the Mississippi River onto the central grasslands. From wooded areas around the Great Lakes came groups that would one day control large stretches of the northern plains—the Blackfeet, Crow, Cheyenne, Arapaho, and several groups of Lakota.

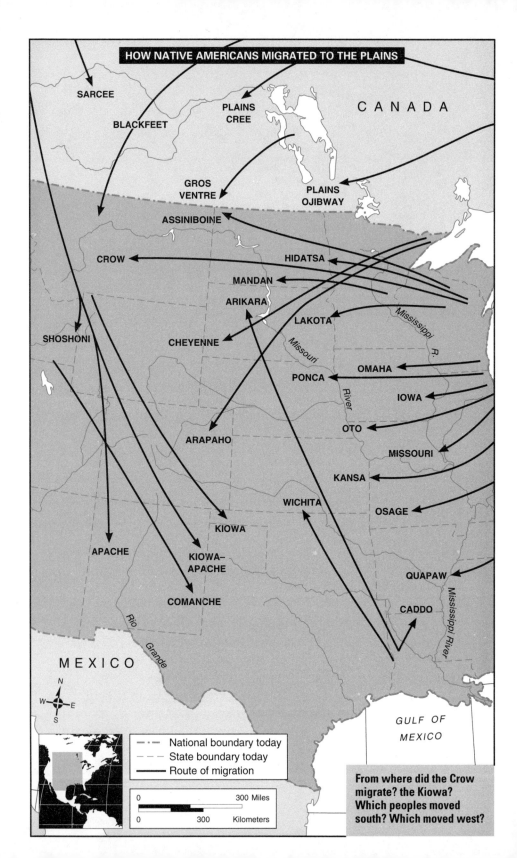

HOW NATIVE AMERICANS MIGRATED TO THE PLAINS

SARCEE

BLACKFEET

PLAINS CREE

GROS VENTRE

PLAINS OJIBWAY

C A N A D A

ASSINIBOINE

CROW

HIDATSA

MANDAN

ARIKARA

LAKOTA

Mississippi R

CHEYENNE

Missouri

SHOSHONI

OMAHA

PONCA

River

IOWA

OTO

ARAPAHO

MISSOURI

KANSA

WICHITA

OSAGE

KIOWA

APACHE

KIOWA–APACHE

COMANCHE

QUAPAW

CADDO

Mississippi River

Rio Grande

MEXICO

N
W E
S

GULF OF MEXICO

--·-- National boundary today

----- State boundary today

—— Route of migration

0   300 Miles

0   300   Kilometers

From where did the Crow migrate? the Kiowa? Which peoples moved south? Which moved west?

This population shift increased rivalries on the plains, as more people competed for the resources of the region. Around 1730, battles took place on the upper plains that showed how intense rivalries had become and how quickly new ways were shaping events. The Plains Shoshoni had heard of the arrival of an animal new to the southern plains—the horse. Apache and Comanche raiders took horses from Hispanic settlers who crossed into their lands from Mexico. The Apache and Comanche soon became highly skilled mounted warriors and hunters.

With this in mind, the Shoshoni hoped to get their own horses to strike at the Blackfeet who had invaded their buffalo lands. Through trade or raid, the Shoshoni gained several of the animals. In 1730, they swept down on a band of Blackfeet, swinging war clubs from the backs of horses. The Blackfeet fled in terror, but not for long. They asked the neighboring Cree to help them battle the "big dogs." The Cree responded by showing the Blackfeet a new weapon—a hollow iron rod that spit out metal balls. The guns, said the Cree, came from French fur traders in Canada. Armed with about 10 of these weapons, a group of Blackfeet and Cree set out to do battle with the Shoshoni. This time, the guns forced the Shoshoni to run.

The two raids convinced the Blackfeet to gain horses and guns of their own. Within a short time, they had mastered use of both. By the late 1700s, the Blackfeet were one of the powerful "horse nations" of the northern plains. The Cheyenne, Lakota, Kiowa, and other Native Americans took to horseback, too. The power of these great horse nations lasted for barely a century. But during that brief time, Native Americans dominated about a million square miles (2.6 million square kilometers) of grasslands, developing a way of life uniquely suited to their surroundings.

TAKING ANOTHER LOOK

1. How did Native Americans organize their lives to fit the environment of the Great Plains?

2. Why was the buffalo important to Plains peoples?

3. *CRITICAL THINKING* How did European settlement of North America affect the lives of Native Americans on the plains?

2 FLOWERING OF THE PLAINS CULTURE

What was life like for members of one of the great horse nations of the plains?

In the mid-1800s, in "the Moon of the Red Cherries" (July), three Lakota scouts rode into camp. They carried important news. "Tell me what you have seen," demanded one of the Lakota leaders. The scouts told of climbing three hills. Behind the first, they spied a small herd of buffalo. Behind the second, they saw an even larger one. Behind the third, said the scouts, "there was nothing but buffalo."

The leaders sent a warrior running through the camp. "Make ready, make haste; your horses make ready! We shall go forth with arrows. Plenty of meat we shall make!" Hunters rushed to grab their best horses. The hunt was on.

Seeking Honor A Lakota leader picked the best hunters from the group. "Today you shall feed the helpless," ordered the leader. "Whatever you kill shall be theirs." The young hunters chosen for this job swelled with pride. It was a great honor to be selected to help other Lakota.

When the band of hunters reached the buffalo herd, someone gave the order to charge: *"Hokay hey!"* In a swirl of dust, mounted Lakota rode into the herd. From the backs of racing horses, they fired arrow after arrow. That day, a young 13-year-old-hunter named Standing Bear made his first kill. *"Yuhoo! Yuhoo!"* shouted the youth over and over.

Off in the distance, 9-year-old Black Elk watched the hunters from his pony. He dreamed of the day when he too could join in a buffalo hunt. That evening, back in camp, Black Elk and the other young boys practiced war games on their ponies. As they knocked each other off onto the ground, each let out a yell of victory: *"Yuhoo!"*

Changing Ways of Life Possession of the horse greatly changed the lives of Native Americans on the plains. In the past, women had slowly dragged most of a family's possessions across the plains on **travois** (trah-VWAH), a net or platform lashed between long wooden poles. Sometimes,

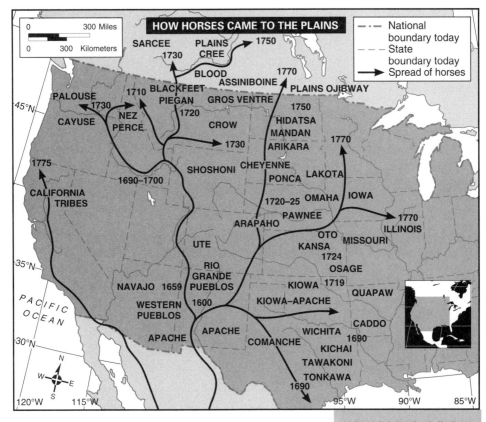

HOW HORSES CAME TO THE PLAINS

- --- National boundary today
- --- State boundary today
- → Spread of horses

0 300 Miles
0 300 Kilometers

SARCEE 1730 — PLAINS CREE — 1750
BLOOD
BLACKFEET — ASSINIBOINE — 1770
PIEGAN — PLAINS OJIBWAY
PALOUSE 1710 1730 — GROS VENTRE
CAYUSE — NEZ PERCE — 1720 — CROW — 1750
1730 — HIDATSA — MANDAN — ARIKARA — 1770
1775
CALIFORNIA TRIBES — SHOSHONI 1690–1700 — CHEYENNE — PONCA — LAKATO
ARAPAHO — OMAHA — IOWA — 1770 ILLINOIS
1720–25
PAWNEE
UTE — OTO — MISSOURI
KANSA 1724
RIO GRANDE PUEBLOS — OSAGE
NAVAJO 1659 — KIOWA 1719 — QUAPAW
WESTERN PUEBLOS 1600 — KIOWA–APACHE
APACHE — APACHE — WICHITA — CADDO 1690
COMANCHE — KICHAI
TAWAKONI
TONKAWA 1690

PACIFIC OCEAN

they used dogs to pull the travois. With horsepower, women no longer had to bend their backs under the weight of heavy loads. Horses could carry far heavier loads on a travois. In addition, they could pull the travois faster and farther.

When did the Assiniboine acquire horses? the Kiowa? Which people were the first to acquire horses?

The use of horses allowed the plains people to carry more possessions with them in their travels. Native Americans of the plains built bigger **tipis,** or cone-shaped tents. They made more clothing, often richly decorated with feathers and quills. Women also packed bigger sacks of food and stored large quantities of **pemmican.** Pemmican was a paste made of pounded dry buffalo meat, fat, and boiled cherries. It was one of the favorite foods on the Plains. "When I think of pemmican," recalled a Crow woman named Pretty Shield, "I grow hungry."

Horses allowed Plains peoples to follow buffalo herds more easily. Hunting from horses was far safer than the old method of crawling in among the herds disguised in furs. Also, fewer warriors were needed for the hunt. This left warriors with free time for other activities.

In battle, most Native Americans sought to display their fighting skills and courage, not to take lives. A warrior won far more respect for **counting coup** (koo), or touching an enemy, than for killing someone. Battle wounds carried only minor honor, while items won during war brought great praise. Many horse soldiers returned home proudly displaying feathered war bonnets or leather shields of enemy nations.

Because Native Americans spent so much time on horseback, strong bonds developed between horse and rider. A great Lakota warrior named Teal Duck recalled dismounting his horse in the middle of a heated battle to ask it for help. "We are in danger," said Teal Duck.

> If you have to run for your life and mine, do your
> best, and if we reach home, I will give you the
> best eagle feather I can find, . . . and you shall be
> painted with the finest paint.

His horse carried him to safety, and Teal Duck kept his word.

Ways of Women and Men The Native American horse-and-buffalo cultures reached their peak on the Great Plains in the 1800s. The most dominant nations of the northern and central plains were the Blackfeet, Crow, Cheyenne, and Lakota. The Comanche, Arapaho, and Kiowa controlled large stretches of the southern plains. From time to time, other nations pushed into the buffalo lands from the west, including the Shoshoni and the Nez Perce (ness PURSE), but they did not control large areas.

Ways of life among these people varied. Yet certain similarities developed among the horse nations. All were nomadic hunting groups, migrating in search of buffalo, or seeking sheltered valleys in wintertime. Social differences grew up, based on a person's hunting skills, spiritual powers, or material wealth. Divisions also existed between men and women. Men tended to be hunters and warriors. Women maintained the camps and organized the frequent moves. In her old age, Pretty Shield proudly recalled the

Native Americans used the horse-drawn travois until the late 1800's. The bent-wood structure on this travois kept small children from falling off.

contributions of Native American women on the plains:

> We women had our children to care for, meat to cook, and to dry, robes to dress, skins to tan, clothes, lodges, and moccasins to make. Besides these things, we not only pitched the lodges, but took them down and packed the horses and travois, when we moved camp. . . . We were busy, especially when we were going to move. I loved to move, even after I was a married woman with children to take care of. Moving made me happy.

Native American cultures of the plains valued highly the accomplishments of women. The products of their labor often carried as much honor as a warrior's deeds in battle. Among the Lakota and Cheyenne, for example, women performed the sacred task of decorating leather with porcupine or bird quills. Acceptance into a quillers' society won great prestige for women in either nation.

The Ways of Children The Native Americans of the plains welcomed the birth of children. As a child's birth neared, a husband often took on his wife's tasks. He carried wood, cooked, and watched their other children. Both parents took part in ceremonies to ensure the child's health.

BLACK ELK SPEAKS

In the spring of 1931, a writer named John Neihardt made his way to Pine Ridge, South Dakota. Neihardt had been granted an interview with 68-year-old Black Elk. Black Elk rarely talked to non-Native Americans. But he sensed that Neihardt might be the person to save his Great Vision for future generations.

The Lakota prepared carefully for the meeting. They dragged pine trees from far away and planted them around Black Elk's cabin. They put up a special tipi painted with sacred symbols.

Using an interpreter, Neihardt and his two daughters, Enid and Hilda, took down Black Elk's every word. The result was a book entitled *Black Elk Speaks*. It has been described by some experts as one of the best expressions of Native American religious beliefs.

Today, more than a half century after its publication, *Black Elk Speaks* is still read by people of varied backgrounds and beliefs. It has been translated into Japanese, Spanish, and Thai, among many other languages.

Upon the birth of a child, the parents prayed for its long life. The Omaha, in what is now Nebraska, sang:

> Ho! Ye Sun, Moon, Stars, all ye that move in the
>   heavens.
> I bid all of you to hear me!
> Into your midst has come a new life.
> Consent ye, I implore [beg]!
> Make its path smooth—then it may reach the
>   brow of the first hill [of life].

At first, boys and girls played together. But as they grew older, boys learned the ways of men, while girls learned the ways of women. The end of childhood for boys arrived with their first buffalo hunt. For most girls, it came with marriage.

Often, parents selected a daughter's husband. Other times, young men courted women with special love songs played on wooden flutes. Even then, however, few marriages took place without the consent of parents. This consent often depended upon proof of bravery or a gift of horses—the basis of a family's wealth.

Great Mystery The religious beliefs of all Native Americans guided their passage through life. Although Native Americans honored the spirit of every living thing, they believed in one higher being. Names included the Great Spirit, Great Silence, and Great Mystery. Native Americans saw evidence of this being in nearly every aspect of life. Explained a member of the Lakota named Brave Buffalo:

> When I was ten years of age, I looked at the land and the rivers, the sky above, and the animals around me and could not fail to realize that they were made by some great power.

Native Americans believed the Great Mystery spoke to them in everyday life and in dreams. Sometimes these dreams were troubling. Later in his life, when he was a long-hair, Black Elk recalled a dream described to him by his father. In it, a holy person called Drinks Water saw all the "four-leggeds" disappear beneath the earth. A strange race of people then wove a spider's web around the Lakota. "When this happens," warned Drinks Water, "you shall live in square gray houses, in a barren land, and beside those gray houses you shall starve."

When Black Elk retold this dream to a writer (see feature), most of the buffalo had vanished from the plains. Black Elk lived in a one-room cabin on land given to the Lakota by the U.S. government. Within a single lifetime, the Plains culture had nearly disappeared.

TAKING ANOTHER LOOK

1. How did possession of the horse change life among Native Americans on the plains?
2. What were some of the different tasks performed by Native American women and men?
3. *CRITICAL THINKING* Based on information in this section, what were some of the most important values among people such as the Lakota

CHAPTER 1: CLOSE UP

1 Buffalo People and Horse Nations

- Native Americans on the Great Plains developed strong ties with the land, taking advantage of whatever resources the region had to offer.
- The existence of huge herds of buffalo led many Native Americans on the Great Plains to develop cultures based on hunting.
- Pressure from settlement forced many Native Americans from woodlands to the east to move out onto the Great Plains.

2 Flowering of the Plains Culture

- The arrival of the horse brought great changes to the hunting cultures of the Plains.
- Use of the horse gave Native Americans the freedom to develop more complex ways of life.
- The accomplishments of Native American women, especially in the arts, were honored as highly as deeds of bravery by men.

WHO, WHAT, WHERE

1. **Who** was Black Elk?
2. **What** natural features make the Great Plains a distinct geographic region?
3. **Where** were the original homelands of the Blackfeet, Cheyenne, and Lakota before they migrated onto the Great Plains?
4. **Who** brought the first horses to the plains?
5. **What** were some of the leading Native American nations on the northern and central plains?
6. **Who** were some of the leading Native American nations on the southern Plains?
7. **What** was pemmican?
8. **What** was "counting coup"?
9. What was the Great Silence?

1. How did Native American life follow the rhythm of the seasons?
2. How did the arrival of Native Americans from the east affect life on the plains?
3. How did use of the horse create cultural changes among Native Americans on the plains?
4. How did women play an important part in shaping the cultures of the great horse nations of the plains?

MAKING CONNECTIONS

1. What was the connection between the abundance of buffalo and the development of social roles within the horse nations?
2. What was the connection between the religious beliefs of Native Americans and their view of nature?

WRITING ABOUT HISTORY

1. Imagine you are a Native American on the plains in the early 1800s. Write a description of how your ancestors lived before the arrival of the horse.
2. Imagine you are a Native American teenager in one of the nations of the plains. Write a series of diary entries that reflect one week of your life. Make sure your entries reflect the traditional roles played by young men and women in Plains culture.
3. Native Americans composed many songs honoring both the buffalo and the horse. Write the lyrics to a song that a Native American woman or man might have composed.
4. In the 1930s, a number of writers interviewed the last generation of Native Americans to have lived freely on the plains. Imagine you are an older Native American such as Black Elk or Pretty Shield. Write a list of things you would want the writer to know about the great horse-and-buffalo cultures in the mid-1800s.

NEW HOME ON THE PLAINS

THINKING ABOUT THE CHAPTER

How did the people of the Five Nations make a new home on the Great Plains after being forced out of their homeland in the southeastern United States?

SECTIONS

1 Trail of Tears

2 A Spirit Unbroken

In 1776, a group of Iroquois (IHR-uh kwoi) from New York State showed up with gifts at Chota—the center of Cherokee government, in the valley of the Tennessee River. The Iroquois presented the Cherokee with several belts known as **wampum**, made of beautiful purple and white shells. These were special war belts, by which the Iroquois were asking the Cherokee to become their allies. The Iroquois wanted the Cherokee to side with the British in the American Revolution, which was just beginning.

Native Americans could thus strike at the American colonists and regain lost land. "We once possessed land almost to the seashore," said one Iroquois, "now [we] have hardly enough ground to stand on."

A Cherokee leader named Dragging Canoe, a bitter foe of the colonists, took the belts. His father, Little Carpenter, and other Cherokee leaders were reluctant to take sides. Wars with the colonists had cost the Cherokee both life and land. Only Nancy Ward, Little Carpenter's niece, spoke strongly for peace.

Both men and women were leaders in the Cherokee nation. Cherokee women took an active

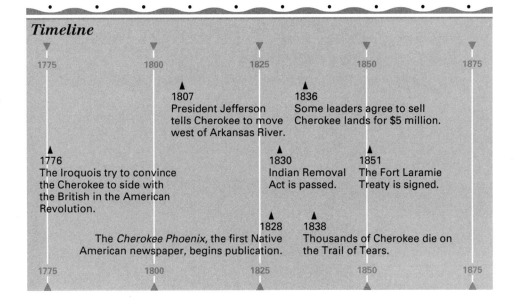

Timeline

1776
The Iroquois try to convince the Cherokee to side with the British in the American Revolution.

1807
President Jefferson tells Cherokee to move west of Arkansas River.

1828
The *Cherokee Phoenix*, the first Native American newspaper, begins publication.

1830
Indian Removal Act is passed.

1836
Some leaders agree to sell Cherokee lands for $5 million.

1838
Thousands of Cherokee die on the Trail of Tears.

1851
The Fort Laramie Treaty is signed.

part in their government. They had the rights to speak and to vote in their councils. Ward had gained respect by avenging the death of her first husband in battle. She later married a non-Native American trader whose name was Ward. Because Ward knew the worlds of both the Cherokee and the colonist, the Cherokee took her advice seriously. Stay out of the war, said Ward. The settlers will probably win.

The Cherokee split. Some sided with the colonists, and some sided with the British. All of them paid dearly. When the American Revolution ended, the Cherokee lost a huge chunk of their land (see map, page 21).

However, relations seemed to improve in 1785, when the new U.S. government sent its first treaty to the Cherokee. Instead of taking away new land, this treaty asked the Cherokee to have "full confidence in the justice of the United States." But such pledges were not met. Settlers soon broke the 1785 treaty and many others that followed. This chapter traces the trail of broken treaties that forced the Cherokee westward to the plains. We will follow the Cherokee in this chapter. However, their fate was shared by their Native American neighbors in the southeastern United States—the Choctaw, Chickasaw, Creek, and Seminole. Together with the Cherokee, they were called by white settlers the Five Civilized Tribes.

1 TRAIL OF TEARS

How were the Cherokee forced to move west?

In 1807, President Thomas Jefferson invited a group of Cherokee to visit Washington, D.C., the nation's new capital. Jefferson greeted the Cherokee warmly. He then asked the Cherokee to exchange part of their homeland for territory west of the Arkansas River. Any Cherokee who refused to go, said Jefferson, should learn the ways of the settlers.

Jefferson's request deeply divided the Cherokee. As pressure over the land issue increased, they began to break up into factions. Some leaders argued that only by giving up their old ways would the Cherokee be able to keep their homeland and share power in the new United States.

New Ways or Old? Thus, many Cherokee learned English. Some accepted Christianity. Most took up the methods of farming used by the settlers and began plowing the land. A few Cherokee became wealthy, and some of them bought enslaved African Americans and built plantations. So many new ways alarmed other Cherokee. Many angry discussions were held and some ended in fistfights.

In 1812, the same U.S. government that had asked the Cherokee to leave their homelands asked them to fight the British. Many Cherokee hoped the government would stop trying to take their lands if the Cherokee proved their loyalty. So they joined with the United States in the War of 1812.

Hundreds of Cherokee served under the command of Tennessee general Andrew Jackson. During one battle, a Cherokee named Junaluska (joo-nah-LOO-skah) saved Jackson's life. Junaluska would live to regret his action. After the War of 1812, Jackson showed no sympathy to his former allies. He devoted himself to removing Native Americans from the southeast. "Build a fire under them," advised Jackson. "When it gets hot enough, they'll move."

Cherokee Unity Most Cherokee resisted resettlement. But some decided to free themselves from conflict with the settlers by moving west. In 1818, a group headed across the Arkansas River. These people, the first Cherokee to head west, became known as the Old Settlers. The majority of Cherokee, however, clung to the remaining part of their homeland. They adopted a constitution and set up a government modeled after that of the United States. Cherokee leaders established their capital at New Echota near present-day Calhoun, Georgia.

A System of Writing Across the Arkansas River, a Cherokee silversmith named Sequoyah (suh-KWOY-uh) was working on a project that one day would become a powerful tool for Cherokee unity. Sequoyah spoke no English and knew little about writing. But he realized that a written Cherokee language would be a powerful tool for communication and education among the Cherokee. He dedicated the remainder of his life to the task of creating a written Cherokee

Which of the nations shown on the map was the last to move west? Which nation traveled the longest distance?

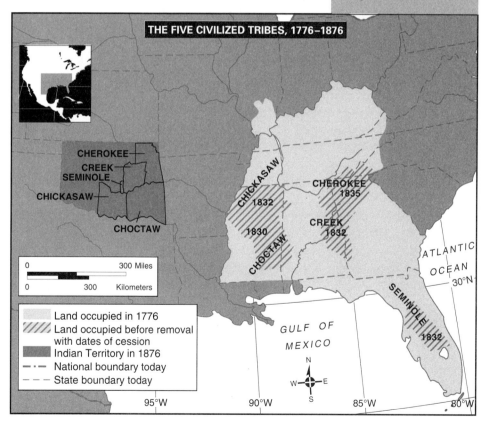

THE FIVE CIVILIZED TRIBES, 1776–1876

CHEROKEE
CREEK
SEMINOLE
CHICKASAW
CHOCTAW

CHICKASAW
1832
CHEROKEE
1835
CHOCTAW
1830
CREEK
1832
SEMINOLE
1832

ATLANTIC OCEAN
30°N

GULF OF MEXICO

0   300 Miles
0   300 Kilometers

Land occupied in 1776
Land occupied before removal with dates of cession
Indian Territory in 1876
National boundary today
State boundary today

N
W   E
S

95°W   90°W   85°W   80°W

language. Sequoyah broke the Cherokee language into 86 syllables, or sounds. He then gave each one a symbol.

Sequoyah carried letters between the Old Settlers and New Echota, proving that the Cherokee "could talk at a distance." Cherokee educators in New Echota matched Sequoyah's symbols to characters in the Greek and Roman alphabets. In 1828, the first Native American newspaper, the *Cherokee Phoenix*, rolled off a press in New Echota. The paper helped to unite Cherokee on both sides of the Mississippi. By 1830, the Cherokee nation had a higher **literacy rate,** or percentage of people able to read, than the United States.

Across the Mississippi Great as they were, these accomplishments did not change the view of those who wanted Native American land in the southeast. Disaster struck in 1829 when Andrew Jackson became President. Jackson had appealed to land-hungry settlers by campaigning on a promise to push Native Americans across the Mississippi. In 1830, Jackson and his supporters narrowly won passage of the Indian Removal Act, a bill ordering the Cherokee, Choctaw, Chickasaw, Creek, and Seminole and almost all other Native Americans in the eastern United States to move into the "Indian Territory." This was a piece of land in what is today the state of Oklahoma (see map, page 21).

Thousands of Native Americans were marched out of the Southeast—some at the point of a bayonet. Cherokee who managed to remain tried to fight the new law. But the settlers lashed out at them. Cherokee in Georgia were beaten and even murdered. The Georgia militia shut down the *Cherokee Phoenix*. Finally, in 1836, a group of Cherokee leaders who sought to end the violence signed a treaty selling Cherokee lands for $5 million. Some Cherokee branded them traitors and swore revenge.

The Cherokee were given two years to move west. Some left fairly soon. Others, led by John Ross, held out. Ross took the 1836 treaty to the Supreme Court, which ruled it unconstitutional. However, the Cherokee victory was short-lived. President Jackson pledged to push the Five Nations out, no matter what the ruling of the U.S. Supreme Court. Junaluska, who had saved Jackson's life, cursed himself for not allowing a bullet to cut Jackson down.

A Tragic March In May 1838, time ran out for the Cherokee. Nearly 17,000 Cherokee still remained in the east. U.S. soldiers pulled men from fields, women from spinning wheels, and children from play forcing them into stockades. The tightly packed stockades soon became disease-ridden death traps. At the same time, throughout the southeastern United States, the Seminole, Creek, Chickasaw, and Choctaw were also being harshly uprooted and held in stockades.

In the fall of 1838, John Ross led his people on a forced journey to Indian Territory. First, the Cherokee suffered under a blazing sun, and people died by the hundreds. Then came the bitter plains winter. Frostbite, hunger, and despair claimed thousands more. Bayonets kept the weary Cherokee moving. Graves lined the trail. Nearly one fourth of the remaining Cherokee nation and many of their slaves died. Among the dead was Quatie, the wife of John Ross.

The Cherokee called the tragic march the Trail Where We Cried, or the Trail of Tears. When it ended, those Cherokee, and the Choctaw, Seminole, Creek, and Chickasaw who also survived the Trail of Tears, faced the overwhelming task of building a new life in a strange land. ,

1. How did the Cherokee try to hold onto their homeland in the southeastern United States?
2. What splits developed among the Cherokee in the years 1776–1836?
3. *CRITICAL THINKING* Some Cherokee fled to the mountains of the southeastern United States rather than move to Indian Territory. What would you have done?

2 A SPIRIT UNBROKEN

How did the Cherokee build a new way of life on the Great Plains?

Angered by the injustice of their removal to Indian Territory, the Cherokee started fighting among themselves. Although still grieving over Quatie, John Ross appealed for unity among the Cherokee. Joining him was Sequoyah. Now in his late 70s, Sequoyah urged the Cherokee to support a new constitution. Its opening words read in part, "We, the people . . . do hereby solemnly . . . agree to form ourselves into one body politic under the style and title of the Cherokee nation."

The work of trying to unify the Cherokee exhausted Sequoyah. While looking for a group of Cherokee living somewhere on the southern plains, to bring them word of the new constitution, he died. He had wanted to deliver one last message: "A great Cherokee nation is rising to the north. Come join us!"

Rebuilding a Nation By the mid-1840s, the Cherokee were united enough to press their grievances against their common enemy—the U.S. government. In 1846, the Cherokee joined together to sign a new treaty with the United States. In the treaty, the United States formally recognized the Cherokee as a nation and agreed to pay the Cherokee for some of their property lost during the removal.

The Cherokee began a remarkable effort to rebuild. They drew up plans for a new capital city called Tahlequah(TAL-uh-kwaw). Soon, brick-and-stone buildings rose above the Oklahoma grasslands. The Cherokee set up an

The Cherokee Female Seminary was founded in 1851. The original structure was destroyed by fire in 1887; the rebuilt school is shown in this photograph.

extensive system of education that included two free high schools—one for boys and one for girls. The Cherokee Female Seminary was known for its educational excellence. At the time, a strong commitment to the education of women was unusual, but it was in keeping with Cherokee tradition.

The Cherokee also reopened their presses. A bilingual newspaper, the *Cherokee Advocate*, printed articles in English and Cherokee. Other presses turned out various books, from the Bible to copies of Cherokee laws and an almanac. By 1855, nearly a million pages a year flowed off Cherokee presses. The Cherokee were justly proud of the unity they had built and the advances they had made.

John Ross and other leaders looked at the landscape of Indian Territory and saw opportunity. But the removal had wiped out many Cherokee. So the Cherokee turned to a source of labor they had used in the east—enslaved African Americans. Soon Cherokee slave traders became a familiar sight in the slave markets of New Orleans. This decision, as you will read in the next chapter, would once again drag the Cherokee into conflict with the U.S. government.

A CONTINUING CUSTOM

"It is customary among [us] to admit women to our councils," explained Little Carpenter to a British official in the mid-1700s. He then wondered why non-Native Americans did not admit women to their councils. He asked, "Are we not all born of women?"

In 1990, the Cherokee elected Wilma Mankiller as their principal chief. Her last name reflects the title given to distant ancestors who achieved honor in battles hundreds of years ago. Today, Chief Mankiller talks about the victory of the Cherokee spirit:

> Despite everything that's happened to our people
> throughout history, we've managed to hang on to
> our culture, we've managed to hang on to our
> sense of being Cherokee. . . . Two hundred years
> from now, people will gather right here in this
> very place, and there will still be a very strong
> Cherokee Nation.

Pressure for Land The Five Civilized Tribes were exiled from their homelands because a land-hungry United States was in the process of removing Native Americans from lands east of the Mississippi. By the mid-1800s, most Native Americans from the woodlands of the eastern United States had been forced to move to the Great Plains.

The Native Americans of the great horse-and-buffalo nations, such as the Sioux or Lakota, Comanche, Cheyenne, and Blackfeet, took a dim view of these events. They were very concerned about the large numbers of Native Americans from the east, such as the Cherokee and Chickasaw, who were now settling on traditional plains hunting grounds. Afraid they would lose their lands, the horse nations sometimes fought with the newly arrived Native Americans.

Pathway to the Pacific In the 1840s and 1850s, non-Native Americans also showed up in Indian Territory. Wagon trains wore deep ruts into the earth as they headed toward Oregon. In 1849, gold-hungry prospectors crossed the plains, rushing to California.

Deadly diseases followed in the tracks of the easterners. Cholera and smallpox claimed thousands of Native American men, women, and children. The wastefulness of settlers also disgusted Native Americans. Settlers chopped down scarce trees and burned them for cooking fires. They shot buffalo and left behind the carcasses. Soon the Native American horse soldiers of the plains, angered by this waste of their precious resource, attacked wagon trains and lone riders alike.

In 1849, the U.S. government set up scattered forts along popular wagon routes. In 1851, the government invited leaders from the most powerful horse-and-buffalo nations to attend a meeting at Fort Laramie, in what is now Wyoming. About 12,000 Native Americans—Lakota, Crow, Cheyenne, Arapaho, Gros Ventre, Assiniboine, Arikara, and Shoshoni—attended. There, these nations signed the Fort Laramie Treaty, or what Native Americans called the Big Treaty. The treaty gave Native Americans a small amount of money in return for allowing travelers to use the wagon routes in peace.

Between 1851 and 1871, the United States and Native Americans signed dozens of treaties. None held. A skirmish between the U.S. Army and the Lakota ended the Big Treaty within four years of its signing. Few other treaties lasted much longer. Settlers were beginning to show increasing interest in lands they had once considered worthless. Native Americans had been told by the U.S. government that the lands west of the Mississippi would be theirs "as long as grass grows, or water runs." By the mid-1800s, Native Americans had good reason to fear this promise would not be kept.

TAKING ANOTHER LOOK

1. How did the Cherokee set up a new life on the Plains?
2. Why did the Cherokee extend the use of enslaved Africans into Indian Territory?
3. *CRITICAL THINKING* Imagine you are a member of one of the horse-and-buffalo cultures. How would you view the arrival of the Cherokee on the plains? Explain.

CHAPTER 2: CLOSE UP

1 Trail of Tears

- The Cherokee adopted many non-Native American ways in an effort to maintain their ancestral homeland in the southeastern United States.
- Cherokee accomplishments in the early 1800s included the development of a written language and the adoption of a constitution.
- Land-hungry settlers and a series of broken treaties with the U.S. government pushed the Cherokee, Creek, Chocktaw, Chickasaw, and Seminole out of the southeast and onto the Great Plains.
- Other Native American groups were also pushed west of the Mississippi River by the U.S. government to Indian Territory, in what is now Oklahoma.

2 A Spirit Unbroken

- The Cherokee overcame deep internal splits to build a united Cherokee nation in what is now Oklahoma.
- The Cherokee were among the first people in the United States to establish a system of public education and include women in that system.
- The arrival of Native Americans from the southeastern United States and increased non-Native American traffic across the plains disrupted the great horse-and-buffalo cultures there.

WHO, WHAT, WHERE

1. **Where** was Chota located?
2. **Who** was Nancy Ward?
3. **Where** did the Old Settlers first move?
4. **Who** was Sequoyah?
5. **What** was the *Cherokee Phoenix*?
6. **Who** was John Ross?
7. **What** was the Trail of Tears?
8. **Where** was Tahlequah?
9. **What** was the Fort Laramie Treaty?

1. What rights and opportunities did Cherokee women have?
2. What promises to the Cherokee did the United States break?
3. How did the Cherokee pattern their government after the United States?
4. How did the Indian Removal Act of 1830 deprive Native Americans of basic human rights?
5. What challenges did the Cherokee face in reestablishing their nation on the plains?
6. Why did Native Americans deeply resent the settlers who began to cross their lands in the 1840s and 1850s?

MAKING CONNECTIONS

1. What was the connection between the development of a system of writing and Cherokee unity?
2. What was the connection between the removal of the Five Civilized Tribes and the arrival of enslaved African Americans on the plains?
3. What was the connection between westward expansion of the United States and increased warfare on the plains?

WRITING ABOUT HISTORY

1. Imagine you are either Dragging Canoe or Nancy Ward. Write a speech in which you respond to the Iroquois request that the Cherokee enter the American Revolution on the side of the British.
2. Write an editorial that might have run in the *Cherokee Phoenix* opposing the 1836 treaty.
3. Imagine you are among the group of Cherokee who accompanied John Ross on the Trail of Tears. Record your experiences on the journey in the form of five diary entries.
4. After Sequoyah died, the Cherokee built a memorial in his honor. Write a speech that might have been delivered in praise of Sequoyah's accomplishments.

THE SHADOW OF CIVIL WAR

THINKING ABOUT THE CHAPTER

How did the Civil War increase pressures on Native Americans on the Plains?

I n early August 1861, a group of Creek and Seminole riders set out from Indian Territory for a meeting with the Wichita and Comanche, two of the most powerful horse nations on the southern plains. A huge Confederate flag and dozens of brightly colored banners streamed in the wind as they rode across the prairie. Three chiefs allied with the Confederate states that had recently seceded from the Union—John Jumper of the Seminole and Motey Kennard and Chilly McIntosh of the Creek—headed the group. With them was a white Confederate agent named Albert Pike.

Pike hoped to convince the Comanche to end their raids on Texas, which was part of the Confederacy. The Confederates could not afford to spare soldiers from the east to protect the Texas frontier. In fact, they hoped to recruit more Native Americans, as they had recruited these Creek and Seminole, to join their cause. Pike offered the Comanche and Wichita lavish gifts in exchange for an end to raids in Texas. He then held out a treaty that placed the Comanche and other Native Americans "under the protection of the Confederate States of America . . . in peace and war forever."

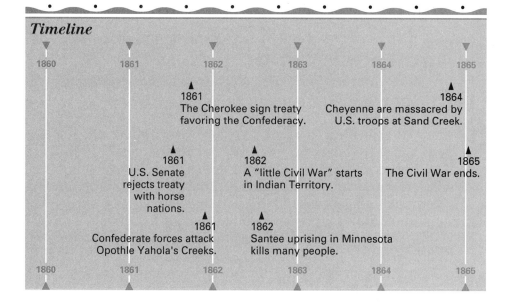

1861
The Cherokee sign treaty favoring the Confederacy.

1864
Cheyenne are massacred by U.S. troops at Sand Creek.

1861
U.S. Senate rejects treaty with horse nations.

1862
A "little Civil War" starts in Indian Territory.

1865
The Civil War ends.

1861
Confederate forces attack Opothle Yahola's Creeks.

1862
Santee uprising in Minnesota kills many people.

No agreement was signed, but news of the Confederate attempt to ally with the horse-and-buffalo nations alarmed U.S. officials. Now *they* tried to persuade Native Americans to join with them. In 1861, President Lincoln invited leaders from the Comanche, Kiowa, Cheyenne, and Arapaho to a meeting at the White House. Lincoln convinced these representatives of the Plains nations to sign yet another treaty with the United States. The U.S. Senate, however, was angry with Lincoln and thought the gifts that he had offered to the Native Americans were too generous, so it refused to approve the treaty. Furious at yet another in a string of broken promises, the Comanche and others attacked U.S. Army posts throughout the southern plains. In response, the United States sent blue-coated federal troops onto the plains.

This chapter explores the impact of the Civil War on the Native Americans of the plains. The war shattered unity among the Five Civilized Tribes. It helped draw the Sioux, Comanche, and other Native American nations into conflict with the U.S. government and opened the door for the government to claim yet more Native American land. This time, however, the land that was taken was land on the plains that had been reserved for Native Americans as a permanent Indian Territory.

1 CHOOSING SIDES

How did the Civil War cause deep divisions among Native Americans on the southern plains?

One morning in June 1861, two months before the meeting between the Confederates and Comanche, John Ross heard a knock at the front door of his stately home, Rose Cottage, in the Indian Territory. As chief of the Cherokee nation, Ross threw open his doors to all visitors. This time, however, Ross opened the door to trouble. The visitor introduced himself as Albert Pike, agent for the Confederacy.

Reopened Wounds Ross was well aware of the violent conflict that was then beginning between the North and the South. He feared that both the Confederacy and the Union would use the war as an excuse to seize Cherokee lands. By 1860, the Cherokee had proven that wealth could be coaxed from the plains. They had plowed through thick prairie grasses to turn more than 100,000 acres (40,500 hectares) into farmland. They grazed more than 300,000

John Ross's first wife, Quatie, died on the Trail of Tears. After settling in Indian Territory, he married Mary Bryan Stapler, with whom he is pictured here.

head of cattle, sheep, horses, and mules on the lush buffalo grass. They cut tons of grass each autumn to feed livestock during the frigid prairie winters.

Ross had taken a stand on the Civil War as soon as he heard of its outbreak. He favored Cherokee **neutrality**, the right to not take sides in the struggle. Ross wrote:

> The Cherokee have properly taken no part in the
> present . . . state of affairs. . . . We do not wish
> our soil to become the battle ground between the
> states, and our homes to be rendered [made] des-
> olate and miserable by the horrors of a civil war.

Yet the Cherokee owned 4,000 enslaved African Americans, and one slaveholder was John Ross. Albert Pike, the Confederate agent, hoped to use this fact to pry Ross away from his neutral position. Pike warned that Union troops might invade Cherokee territory to free the enslaved African Americans. But Ross stood firm:

> The Cherokees are . . . your friends. But we do
> not wish to be brought into feuds between your-
> selves and your Northern Brethren. Our wish is
> for peace.

Some other leaders of the nations that had been forced onto the plains disagreed with Ross. The Civil War re-opened all the old wounds suffered at the time of their expulsion from the southeast. One leader, a Cherokee named Stand Watie, called for close alliance with the Confederacy, to protect slavery. The split widened when Watie raised a Cherokee cavalry to fight for the Confederacy. Other Native Americans who did not own slaves lined up behind Ross for neutrality. Some still burned with resentment over the way they had been treated in the South, and they supported the Union. Others, like the Seminole, had offered a refuge in Florida for escaped African American slaves. Many Seminole had African Americans as relatives.

Ross clung to hopes of peace. But Confederate states bordered the Five Civilized Tribes on three sides. Also, in 1861, the tide of war was running in favor of the South. Ross worried that events might soon force him from power, putting the hot-tempered Watie in charge. So, in October 1861, Ross undercut Watie's power by summoning Albert

Pike. He agreed to sign a treaty favorable to the South. In a tension-filled public ceremony, Ross and Watie shook hands. The Cherokee had now been sucked into the turmoil of the Civil War.

Split Among the Creek. News of Ross's decision stunned Opothle Yahola (oh-PA-thih-luh YAH-hoh-lah). The 80-year-old Creek chief could not forgive the Southerners for expelling his people. He remembered the suffering of the march across the plains in the 1830s. He burned with rage when two of his fellow Creek chiefs, Motey Kennard and Chilly McIntosh, signed a treaty with Albert Pike. In a letter smuggled through Confederate lines, Opothle Yahola pleaded with President Lincoln for help:

> Now the wolf has come. Men who are strangers
> tread our soil. Our children are frightened and
> mothers cannot sleep for fear.

To avoid war, Opothle Yahola moved his followers to a distant camp at the southwestern edge of Creek territory. He urged other proneutrality or pro-Union supporters to join him. Nearly half the Seminole and many runaway enslaved African Americans took up Opothle Yahola's offer.

In late October, Confederate agent Douglas Cooper visited the camp. He saw many old people and infants, but what impressed him most were the more than 1,500 armed Creek, Seminole, and African Americans. When Opothle Yahola refused to disarm his followers, Cooper made a vow to "drive him and his party from the country."

In November, Opothle Yahola's followers left their camp, trying to find the protection of Union troops. Confederate forces—including Choctaw, Creek, Chickasaw, and Cherokee—followed closely. There were a few skirmishes. Then, on the day after Christmas 1861, the Confederate forces attacked and soon had the upper hand.

Rather than surrender, Opothle Yahola retreated, under the cover of a blizzard, in the direction of Union-occupied Kansas. Just when his band thought they were safe, they heard the clatter of hooves. In full charge, Stand Watie and his Cherokee cavalry cut through the group, killing many and scattering the survivors into the freezing rain and snow. Recalled one Seminole chief:

At that battle we lost everything we possessed, everything to take care of our women and children with, and all that we had. . . . We left them [fallen loved ones] in cold blood by the wayside.

After a long march, the survivors reached Kansas. Here they slept on the icy ground, often without the cover of blankets. Many froze to death, including Opothle Yahola's daughter. In April 1862, Union supplies arrived. So did Union recruiters, who asked Native American and African American survivors of the march to join them in battle against the Confederates in the Indian Territory.

A "Little Civil War" In July, Union troops, including Union supporters within the Five Nations, made their way into the Indian Territory. In the battles that followed, thousands of Seminole, Creek, Chickasaw, Cherokee, and Choctaw fought for the Union. Thousands of others, however, fought for the Confederacy. A "little Civil War" was fought in the Indian Territory after 1862.

At one point, a string of Confederate victories in the eastern part of the country led to the withdrawal of most

Some Native Americans fought with the Union. Col. Ely Parker (far right), a Seneca, served as an aide to Union commander U.S. Grant (center, wearing hat).

Union troops from thc Indian Territory. The Confederates, including Stand Watie's unit, plunged back into the region. They set fire to the Cherokee capital at Tahlequah, slaughtered stock, and looted homes. Hundreds of houses, including John Ross's Rose Cottage, went up in flames. Many Native Americans and African Americans fled across the plains toward Kansas. Some never reached safety, dying of hunger along the way. Many of those who managed to reach Kansas enlisted in the Union army and were sent to fight in Arkansas.

Reconstruction In 1865, the Civil War finally ended. The last Confederate officer to hand over his sword was Stand Watie. That year, Native American refugees and many newly freed African Americans returned to the Indian Territory. Like much of the defeated South, that land was a wasteland of burnt cabins and weed-filled fields.

Although many Cherokee, Creek, Choctaw, Chickasaw, and Seminole had remained loyal to the Union, all suffered after the war. Federal officials voided all past treaties. The U.S. government seized huge areas of their land and gave it to other Native Americans, such as the Shawnee, who were being pushed westward by the tide of settlement.

Except for a short visit to Tahlequah, John Ross spent the last years of his life in Washington, D.C. He had lost his home and two sons to the war. Although filled with grief, he battled for justice for his people. In his last years, Ross secured two triumphs. He protected the independence of the Cherokee as a nation. He also fought off efforts by railroads to cut across Cherokee land. In April 1866, as Ross lay dying, he dictated a last speech to his people:

> I am an old man and have served my people and
> the government of the United States . . . for over
> 50 years. My people have kept me in the harness.
> . . . I have never deceived them. . . . I have done
> the best I could, and today upon this bed of sickness, my heart approves of all I have done.

The battle for Native American lands was shifting elsewhere on the plains. The federal government now sought to remove the horse nations to small land holdings similar to those of the Five Civilized Tribes. Far to the north, in Minnesota, the spark of discontent had already been ignited among the Sioux.

TAKING ANOTHER LOOK

1. What events led the Cherokee into the Civil War?
2. Why did some members of the Five Civilized Tribes oppose the Confederacy?
3. *CRITICAL THINKING* Imagine you are John Ross in 1866. What arguments would you use to convince federal officials to treat the Cherokee fairly?

2 SORROW ON THE NORTHERN PLAINS

How did the Civil War bring sorrow and violence to Native Americans on the northern plains?

In 1861, the Santee Sioux of Minnesota watched as federal troops marched out of forts headed for Civil War battlefronts in the South. The absence of troops fueled rumors among the Santee. "It was said the North would be whipped," recalled a Santee chief named Big Eagle.

Many Santee yearned for a chance to undo the wrongs dealt them by the U.S. government. First, they felt that the United States had cheated them out of most of their hunting grounds. This affected their whole way of life. Now, they found themselves crowded onto a **reservation**, land set aside by the government, at the northern end of the Minnesota River. The Santee received payment in gold coins each year for their lost lands. But the payment amounted to little more than $15 a year per person. "It began to be whispered," said Big Eagle, "that now would be a good time to go to war . . . and get back our lands."

Broken Promises During the summer of 1862, a series of disasters hit the Santee. Cutworms ruined their corn crop. Newly arrived settlers pressed in from all sides. The cleared farmland caused game to migrate to more wooded areas, leaving little for the Santee to hunt. The final blow came in July. The payment of gold coins failed to arrive on time. The Santee had been depending on the money to buy food. Now some traders at the reservation refused to sell the Santee food on credit, and some who did charged high prices. Many Santee were close to starvation.

On August 15, a chief named Little Crow and other Santee had a meeting with federal agent Thomas Galbraith and some traders. "The money is ours," pointed out Little Crow, "but we cannot get it." He then gestured at the piles of food in the agency.

> We have no food, but here are these stores, filled with food. We ask that you, the agent, make some arrangement by which we can get food from the stores . . . .When men are hungry they help themselves.

Galbraith turned to a group of traders present at the meeting. "Well," he said, "it's up to you now. What will you do?" One of the traders, Andrew Myrick, turned angrily to leave the building. "So far as I am concerned," Myrick said, "if they are hungry, let them eat grass!"

Myrick's cruel remark humiliated the Santee, who had humbled themselves to ask for food. Little Crow was stunned by Myrick's response. The Santee around Little Crow were shamed and enraged.

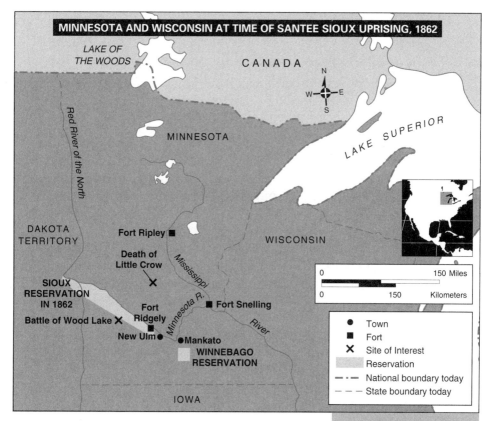

MINNESOTA AND WISCONSIN AT TIME OF SANTEE SIOUX UPRISING, 1862

LAKE OF THE WOODS

CANADA

MINNESOTA

LAKE SUPERIOR

Red River of the North

DAKOTA TERRITORY

Fort Ripley ■

WISCONSIN

Death of Little Crow ✕

SIOUX RESERVATION IN 1862

Mississippi

Fort Ridgely

■ Fort Snelling

Battle of Wood Lake ✕

Minnesota R.

River

New Ulm ●

● Mankato

WINNEBAGO RESERVATION

IOWA

0 ——————— 150 Miles
0 ——————— 150 Kilometers

● Town
■ Fort
✕ Site of Interest
▨ Reservation
— · — National boundary today
— — — State boundary today

A Call for War Only a spark was needed to set off violence. The spark came on the evening of August 17. That night, four Santee youths, who had been out unsuccessfully hunting, wandered up to a settler's house. Here they spied a pile of hen's eggs. One youth dared another to steal the eggs. When the youth hesitated, the other taunted: "You are afraid to take even an egg . . . though you are half-starved. Yes, you are a coward, and I will tell everybody."

Stung by the insult, the youth boasted he would not only steal the eggs. He would also kill the settlers inside the house. But, he said, the others had to help. The four youths shot a total of five people. Then, they stole some horses and rode off into the night.

Hearing of the murders, a group of Santee awakened Little Crow. He found that most of the Santee supported the youths. The time had come for war, they said. Little Crow hesitated, warning:

Along what body of water was the Santee Sioux reservation located? What fort was closest to the reservation?

We are only little herds of buffalo left scattered. . . .
The white men are like the locusts when they fly
so thick that the whole sky is a snowstorm. . . .
Kill one—two—ten, and ten times ten will come
to kill you.

But angry Santee warriors refused to listen. One Santee called Little Crow a coward. Little Crow jumped to his feet. "You will die like rabbits," he announced. "But Little Crow is not a coward. He will die with you!"

Bloodshed The Santee uprising caught settlers by surprise. Before it was over, the Santee killed some 800 men, women, and children in attacks on scattered forts and on settlements at Fort Ridgely and New Ulm. The brutal slayings led the governor of Minnesota to order General Henry Hastings Sibley to gather a force to put down the rising. In hand-to-hand fighting, the Santee could match any rivals. But Sibley came armed with cannon and several newly invented machine guns, and defeated the Santee at the Battle of Wood Lake and several smaller fights.

By the end of September, Sibley had rounded up or killed most of the Santee fighters. A military commission ordered the execution of 303 Santee. However, most of the Santee sentenced to death had not actually been connected with any violent crime. When news of the sentences reached President Lincoln, he ordered an investigation, which reduced the number of death sentences to 38. In the largest mass execution in U.S. history, most of the 38 were hanged at Mankato, Minnesota. Little Crow, who had escaped earlier, was shot by a settler the following July.

Bitter Aftermath For the U.S. government, the Santee rising provided an excuse to seize the last Santee lands. In March 1862, the government ordered the survivors to a reservation along Crow Creek, a tributary of the Missouri. This barren land lacked rain, wild game, and even clean drinking water. Fewer than 1,000 Santee lived through their first winter on the northern plains.

A young member of the Lakota Sioux visited his Santee kin at the time. He heard tales of settlers' greed and broken promises. If the blue-coated troops dared attack the Lakota,

vowed the visitor, he would fight. His name was Tatanka Iyotaka (tah-TAHN-kah EE-oh-tah-kah), or Sitting Bull.

Little Crow had visited Washington, D.C. in 1858 for treaty negotiations in which the Santee lost a large piece of their land. This photograph was taken on that trip.

Attack on the Cheyenne By 1864, a large number of U.S. Army troops patrolled the Plains. Most were responsible for protecting settlers using trails between Union states in the east and California. A flood of settlers over the trails had resulted in a wave of Native American attacks on wagon trains and stagecoach stations. Many settlers, made fearful by the Santee conflict, argued that these troops should be used to solve the so-called Indian problem by destroying their military power.

Two who felt this way were John Evans, governor of the Colorado Territory, and Colonel John M. Chivington, leader of the Colorado cavalry. Evans wanted the Cheyenne

SHARED LESSONS IN EQUALITY

For about 200 years, the history of the nations that whites called the Five Civilized Tribes has been closely entwined with African American history. As you have read, those nations took up settled farming when they were living in the southeast late in the 18th century, and some farmers used enslaved African Americans to work the farms. But most members of those nations had no slaves. Many opposed slavery, and many, in particular the Seminole of Florida, offered a friendly refuge to escaped slaves.

African Americans accompanied the five nations on the Trail of Tears, and many died with them. Many African Americans considered themselves members in full standing of the five nations. For example, O. S. Fox, an African American, was editor of the *Cherokee Afro-American Advocate.*

Each culture enriched the other. When slavery was abolished, African Americans followed the example of the Cherokee in setting up schools on Native American lands.

Some members of the five nations, such as the Chickasaw and Choctaw, resisted extending citizenship to African Americans until the end of the 19th century. Others, such as the Seminole, offered it right away. On the whole, however, African Americans found far greater opportunity among the Native Americans than in the rest of the country. In fact, at the end of the Civil War, many formerly enslaved African Americans living in the Southeast trekked to the Indian Territory.

This cultural sharing has continued in modern times. In the 1950s, African Americans started a civil rights movement that rocked the United States. Their example inspired Native Americans to launch their own rights movement, sharing many of the same goals and tactics as the African American movement.

and Arapaho of Colorado moved to reservations. He seized on the raids to order Colonel Chivington into the field.

On November 28, 1864, Chivington learned of a Cheyenne and Arapaho camp along Sand Creek. He ordered African American scout James Beckwourth to take him there. At first, Beckwourth refused to betray his Native American friends, but Chivington threatened to hang him. Beckwourth reluctantly agreed, but he went as slowly as he could. So Chivington turned to Robert Bent, son of a settler and a Cheyenne woman, and ordered him to lead his force to the Sand Creek encampment.

Blood on the Plains Two of the leaders at the Cheyenne camp at Sand Creek favored peace with the settlers. Black Kettle and White Antelope had both attended the 1861 meeting hosted at the White House (see page 31). Both proudly wore medals given to them by President Lincoln. When Black Kettle saw Chivington's soldiers approaching in full battle formation, he put up a white flag of surrender.

The 70-year-old White Antelope walked toward the soldiers shouting "Stop! Stop!" Chivington ordered his men to load rifles and fire. White Antelope folded his arms and began to sing a death song—special words saved by each Native American for moments of great courage.

Nothing lives long
Only the earth and the mountains.

A rain of bullets struck White Antelope down. Chivington then ordered a full charge into the stunned camp. In the slaughter that followed, most of the Cheyenne leaders who favored peace fell dead. Though Black Kettle managed to escape, his wife and infant granddaughter did not. Testimony by Robert Bent helped convince Congress to label the incident a massacre by federal troops. But words did little to calm Cheyenne hatred. The deaths at Sand Creek drove the Cheyenne into an alliance with the Lakota. Two of the most powerful horse nations on the northern plains now vowed to fight the U.S. government to the death.

TAKING ANOTHER LOOK

1. What events led up to the Santee conflict?
2. How did the attack on Sand Creek help end hopes for peace on the plains?
3. *CRITICAL THINKING* What was the relationship between the Santee rising and the Sand Creek massacre?

CHAPTER 3: CLOSE UP

KEY IDEAS

1 Choosing Sides

- The Civil War renewed old divisions among members of the Cherokee, Creek, Chickasaw, Choctaw, and Seminole as North and South tried to get them to take sides.
- Because of early Confederate victories and shared borders with the Confederacy, the Cherokee under John Ross signed a treaty with the Confederates.
- Some members of the Five Civilized Tribes resisted the Confederates at great loss of life and property.
- After the war, the U.S. government scrapped treaties with the five nations and seized more of their lands.

2 Sorrow on the Northern Plains

- A series of broken promises by the federal government triggered a massive uprising among the Santee Sioux.
- The Santee rising opened the door for the federal government to relocate the Santee on the plains.
- Chivington's attack on pro-Union Cheyenne at Sand Creek helped end hopes that the U.S. government and the horse nations of the northern plains would settle their differences peacefully.

WHO, WHAT, WHERE

1. **Who** was Opothle Yahola?
2. **Where** did Opothle Yahola lead his people for safety?
3. **Where** did John Ross spend his dying days?
4. **What** Native American nations received lands seized from the Cherokee, Creek, Chickasaw, Choctaw, and Seminole?
5. **Where** did the Santee originally live?
6. **Who** was Little Crow?
7. **Where** did the federal government send the Santee Sioux after the 1862 uprising?
8. **Who** was Black Kettle?
9. **What** happened at Sand Creek?

UNDERSTANDING THE CHAPTER

1. Why did John Ross try to follow a policy of neutrality?
2. How did the Civil War further disrupt the lives of the Cherokee, Creek, Chickasaw, Choctaw, and Seminole?
3. What factors contributed to the outbreak of conflict between the Santee and nearby settlers?
4. Why did the example of the Santee inspire other Sioux nations to resist the U.S. government?
5. How did the Civil War increase federal efforts to push the horse nations onto reservations?

MAKING CONNECTIONS

1. What was the connection between Stand Watie's actions and John Ross's signing of a treaty favorable to the South?
2. What was the connection between the Civil War and the Santee uprising?
3. What was the connection between the Civil War and federal interest in keeping the trails to California open?

WRITING ABOUT HISTORY

1. Imagine you are an editor for the *Cherokee Advocate.* Write an article, either pro or con, about John Ross's decision to sign a treaty with Albert Pike.
2. Robert Bent, the son of a settler and a Cheyenne woman, was ordered to lead Colonel Chivington's troops to the Sand Creek Encampment. Compose a letter that he might have written to his mother about the incident.
3. Imagine you are a member of the Cheyenne who has been requested to testify about events at Sand Creek. Write a speech that you might deliver before Congress.
4. Imagine you are a Seminole who joined Opothle Yahole's camp. Write five diary entries about life at the camp and your position on the Civil War.

CHAPTER 4

STRUGGLE FOR THE SOUTHERN PLAINS

THINKING ABOUT THE CHAPTER

Why did Native Americans and U.S. troops battle on the southern plains in the 1860s and 1870s?

I n 1866, the Cheyenne still burned with resentment at the memory of the Sand Creek Massacre. Their anger increased at the sight of crews laying tracks across the prairie for the Kansas Pacific Railroad. "We will not have the wagons which make a noise [steam engines] in the hunting grounds of the buffalo," warned a southern Cheyenne called Roman Nose. To drive home his point, Roman Nose led 500 **Dog Soldiers**, a band of Cheyenne famed for bravery, against the invaders. They attacked track-laying crews and built bonfires out of telegraph poles.

SECTIONS

1 Defeat of the Dog Soldiers

2 War to Save the Buffalo

In "the Moon of the Red Grass Appearing" (April) 1867, a veteran of the Civil War named General Winfield Hancock marched 1,400 blue-coated U.S. Army troops into western Kansas. He demanded a meeting with the leaders of the Dog Soldiers. Three chiefs—Tall Bull, Bull Bear, and White Horse— agreed to talk with him. Roman Nose did not. "Why is Roman Nose not here?" asked Hancock. Tall Bull tried to sidestep the question by saying that Roman Nose was not a chief. Hancock exploded. "If Roman Nose will not come to me I will go to him," he thundered. "I will march my troops to your village tomorrow."

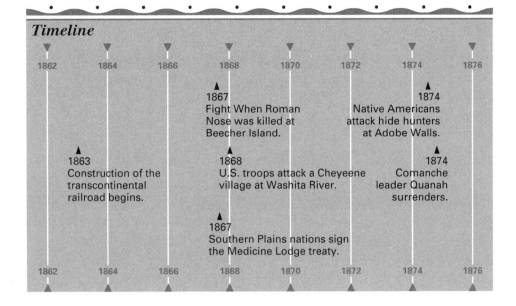

Timeline

1862 — 1864 — 1866 — 1868 — 1870 — 1872 — 1874 — 1876

1867
Fight When Roman Nose was killed at Beecher Island.

1874
Native Americans attack hide hunters at Adobe Walls.

1863
Construction of the transcontinental railroad begins.

1868
U.S. troops attack a Cheyeene village at Washita River.

1874
Comanche leader Quanah surrenders.

1867
Southern Plains nations sign the Medicine Lodge treaty.

Roman Nose had no wish to see U.S. troops come near another Cheyenne village. He rode out to meet Hancock, after sending the women and children out of the camp onto the plains, where they might be safer. Roman Nose would not risk riding into a trap. He formed some 300 Dog Soldiers into a line more than a mile [1.6 kilometers] wide and rode off to see Hancock.

When the armies met, Roman Nose rode up to Hancock and stared directly at him. "Do you want peace or war?" asked Hancock. Roman Nose wanted to kill Hancock, but the other chiefs restrained him. "We do not want war," Roman Nose replied.

Hancock demanded that the women and children be brought back to camp before talks could continue. This made the Native American leaders even more suspicious. When the meeting ended, the Cheyenne slipped away to join the women and children and move further north. Two days later, Hancock sent a cavalry officer named George Armstrong Custer in pursuit of the Cheyenne.

This chapter describes efforts by the federal government to gain control of lands on the lower plains held by the southern Cheyenne and other Native Americans. The struggle lasted from the 1860s to roughly 1880. When it ended, the horse-and-buffalo culture of the plains had ceased to exist.

1 DEFEAT OF THE DOG SOLDIERS
What events led to the defeat of the southern Cheyenne?

As Custer headed out after the Cheyenne, Hancock set fire to their abandoned camp. The flames burned nearly everything the Native Americans owned. The Cheyenne now believed they had narrowly escaped another massacre, and war erupted on the southern plains.

The Dog Soldiers led Custer on a far-flung chase. Sometimes, they hid out among their cousins, the Northern Cheyenne, or their allies, the Lakota. At other times, they galloped their horses across the southern prairies, leaving Custer and his troops far behind in a trail of dust. Raids by the Cheyenne and other Native Americans nearly stopped the traffic of settlers and freight across the lower Great Plains. Late in 1867, government officials decided to make a new effort at convincing the southern nations to accept a peace treaty—and life on reservations.

The Medicine Lodge Treaty In "the Moon of the Changing Season" (October), some 4,000 Native Americans gathered at Medicine Lodge Creek. Their tipis and horses filled the valley, some 60 miles [96 kilometers] south of Fort Larned in Kansas. U.S. Army troops arrived with a battery of rapid-firing Gatling guns—early machine guns—and 30 wagons jammed with gifts. Native Americans and U.S. troops alike strutted around in full battle array. Newspaper reporters from eastern states scribbled notes and set up cameras. "Why do you try to catch my shadow?" snapped one Native American as he smashed a camera to the ground.

The meeting drew leaders from some of the most powerful nations on the southern plains—Arapaho, Kiowa, Comanche, Cheyenne, and prairie Apache. On October 26, the Cheyenne Dog Soldiers appeared on a ridge in the distance. One of them sounded a bugle, and nearly 500 Dog Soldiers whipped their horses into a full gallop. Battle cries and scattered rifle shots filled the air as the pride of the Cheyenne nation splashed across the creek and into the camp.

A few days later, talks began. Federal officials presented a peace plan that called for Native Americans to stop all attacks on the railroads. In exchange, the government offered the Native Americans a great reservation in Indian Territory south of the Arkansas River (see map) and annual payments of goods for 30 years. Soldiers stacked up piles of calico cloth, pants, coats, hats, guns, and ammunition to show the government's generosity. Officials urged Native Americans to take up farming on the new reservation, but few listened. Instead, the Native Americans were most interested in a promise that they could hunt on the reservation and lands nearby for as long as the buffalo ran.

One nation after another signed what became known as the Medicine Lodge Treaty. The Cheyenne split, with supporters of peace, such as Black Kettle, favoring the treaty and the Dog Soldiers opposing it. Federal officials believed the treaty would be useless unless the Dog Soldiers agreed to it. Finally, Tall Bull, White Horse, and Bull Bear grudgingly put their marks on the document. Bull Bear pressed his pen so hard

On what river did the Beecher Island battle take place? What U.S. forts were located in Indian Territory?

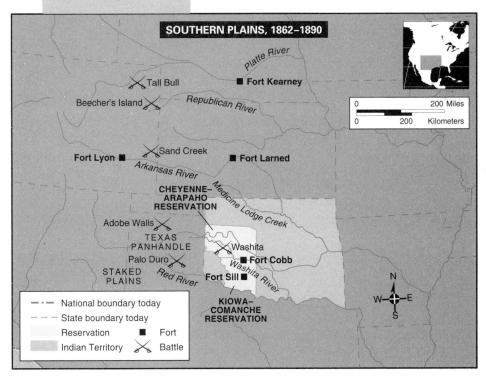

SOUTHERN PLAINS, 1862–1890

Platte River

Tall Bull

Fort Kearney

Beecher's Island

Republican River

0   200 Miles
0   200   Kilometers

Fort Lyon

Sand Creek

Fort Larned

Arkansas River

CHEYENNE–ARAPAHO RESERVATION

Medicine Lodge Creek

Adobe Walls

TEXAS PANHANDLE

Washita

Palo Duro

Fort Cobb

STAKED PLAINS

Red River

Washita River

Fort Sill

N
W—E
S

KIOWA–COMANCHE RESERVATION

—·— National boundary today
— — State boundary today
Reservation   ■ Fort
Indian Territory   ✕ Battle

that it nearly tore through the paper. He said he wanted to be sure the U.S. President saw his mark. Roman Nose, however, refused to sign. One violation of the treaty by the government, warned Roman Nose, and the Dog Soldiers would again take up their war lances.

When Roman Nose Was Killed The treaty lasted no longer than most others negotiated with the federal government. In August 1868, a dispute led some Cheyenne to raid a village of the Kaw nation. As a result, government officials at Fort Larned refused to turn over to the Cheyenne guns and ammunition that had been promised by the treaty. Cheyenne anger at this refusal led the officials to rethink their decision, but the change came too late. A band of Cheyenne warriors had already attacked a non-Native American settlement.

General Philip Sheridan, the new commander on the plains, seized on this incident as a reason for launching all-out war. While he readied his troops, Sheridan recruited a band of buckskin-clad civilians to patrol western Kansas under the guidance of a few army officers. In "the Moon When the Deer Paw the Earth" (September), the group ran into some 700 Dog Soldiers and their allies from the Oglala. The group quickly dug a defensive position on an island in the Arickaree Fork of the Republican River, just over the Colorado line (see map, page 49).

The Dog Soldiers charged the island twice and were driven back by heavy rifle fire each time. On the third charge of the Dog Soldiers, a bullet pierced through Roman Nose's bone-and-leather chest plate, and by evening, he lay dead.

Badly shaken by the loss of Roman Nose, the Dog Soldiers laid siege to the island. Although their food ran out, the civilians held on for nine days, until help finally arrived in the form of the 10th U.S. Cavalry. This was an army unit made up of African American soldiers assigned to the plains. Native Americans called them Buffalo Soldiers. The Dog Soldiers retreated at the sight of these fresh troops. U.S. soldiers called the fight the Battle of Beecher Island, after a fallen officer. Native Americans remembered it as the Fight When Roman Nose Was Killed.

The Washita Massacre By the winter of 1868–69, General Sheridan was ready to begin a campaign to drive all Native Americans of the lower plains into Indian Territory. "We have now selected . . . reservations for all," announced Sheridan. "All who cling to their old hunting grounds are hostile and will remain so till killed off." Sheridan ordered George Armstrong Custer to move south with the 7th Cavalry and destroy the villages of all Native Americans who had not moved near Fort Cobb, in southern Indian Territory.

Custer found one such village in the valley of the Washita River. Its leader was Black Kettle, who had survived the Sand Creek Massacre. Black Kettle had tried to move to Fort Cobb, but the army commander there had refused him permission.

In the early hours of November 27, 1868, Custer's troops moved into place around the village. A Native American woman caught sight of them. "Soldiers! Soldiers!" she screamed. A bugle

The U.S. Army claimed to have killed 103 Native American warriors in the fighting at the Washita. The Cheyenne said they lost 38 men, women, and children.

sounded, and rifle shots rang out. Black Kettle stumbled from bed, grabbing a pistol, but a bullet cut him down before he was far from his tipi. Within minutes, Custer's troops wiped out nearly the entire village. Custer saw the fight as a major victory. Native Americans saw it as a second Sand Creek Massacre.

Surrender The rest of the winter brought more disaster for the southern Cheyenne. U.S. troops pursued them relentlessly. Survivors of battles moved to U.S. Army posts to await assignment to reservations.

Some Dog Soldiers, led by Tall Bull, set out for the northern plains but never reached them. In 1869, in "the Moon When the Cherries Are Ripe" (July), U.S. troops attacked them near the Platte River in Colorado. The Dog Soldiers retreated with their families into a ravine. Here, Tall Bull and the other warriors fought to the death. The once-powerful Dog Soldiers were no longer a force on the plains.

TAKING ANOTHER LOOK

1. Why did the Dog Soldiers take up arms in 1866?

2. What did the Medicine Lodge Treaty promise Native Americans of the lower plains?

3. *CRITICAL THINKING* Imagine that you are a Cheyenne Dog Soldier. How would you respond to General Sheridan's statement on page 51?

2 WAR TO SAVE THE BUFFALO
How did destruction of the buffalo herds affect the Kiowa and Comanche?

At the 1867 meeting at Medicine Lodge Creek, a chief among the Kwahadi (KWAH-hah-duh) band of Comanche had a warning for the U.S. government: "Tell the white chiefs that Kwahadi are warriors and will surrender when the blue coats come and whip us." These strong words came from the son of a Comanche man and a white woman named Cynthia Ann Parker. The Kwahadi had kidnapped

Parker as a child and raised her as a Comanche. She left the Comanche only when non-Native Americans burst into a Kwahadi camp and forced her away. A legend says that Parker never smiled again. Her son never gave up his mother's pet name for him: Quanah, "little fragrant one." As an adult, Quanah led the Kwahadi in a final series of wars to save the buffalo ranges of the southern plains.

The Hide Hunters Destruction of the vast buffalo herds came swiftly. In 1863, construction of the first transcontinental railroad began. Railroad companies hired hunters to shoot buffalo to feed the construction crews. When the railroad line was completed, so-called sport hunters sometimes rode the trains, firing on the herds from the windows.

Then, "buffalo fever" swept the eastern states. People wanted buffalo skins for blankets and rugs. Restaurant-goers craved a new delicacy—smoked buffalo tongue. Tanners found buffalo hides made a better leather than cowhides. A Kiowa woman named Old Lady Horse recalled what happened next:

> Then the white men hired hunters to do nothing
> but kill the buffalo. Up and down the plains those
> men ranged, shooting sometimes as many as a
> hundred buffalo a day. Behind them came the
> skinners with their wagons. They piled the hides
> and bones into their wagons . . . and took their
> loads to the new railroad stations. . . . Sometimes
> there would be a pile of bones as high as a man,
> stretching a mile along the railroad track.

By 1873, some parts of the prairie, seen from a distance, looked white from the bleached bones of slaughtered buffalo. The air hung heavy with the smell of rotting carcasses. As herds were hunted out on the open plains, the hide hunters looked eagerly toward the buffalo ranges promised to Native Americans under the Medicine Lodge Treaty. "The buffalo saw that their day was over," explained Old Lady Horse. "They could no longer protect their people." But Native Americans such as Quanah decided they could do something to protect the buffalo and their own ways of life. They could fight.

Crossing the Red River The Medicine Lodge Treaty forbade Native Americans from crossing the Red River into Texas. But some Kiowa and Comanche hunters ignored the treaty. Small bands crossed the river, hunting buffalo or raiding horses as far south as Mexico. "I don't want to settle," said Satanta, a fiery Kiowa chief. "I love to roam over the prairie."

In 1871, Satanta openly defied the treaty by attacking a wagon train in Texas. He then boasted about the attack to a U.S. Army officer. Only the protests of reformers friendly to Native Americans saved Satanta from execution.

Quanah freely roamed the southern plains, too. The Kwahadi nation had never signed a treaty. Nor would they, vowed Quanah. Kwahadi raids across the Red River led the U.S. Army to build a string of forts along the southern edge of the Staked Plains, the southern boundary of Indian Terri-

tory. But Quanah simply swung around the forts and headed into Texas.

Attack at Adobe Walls Close bonds had developed between the Kiowa and Comanche. The free-spirited hunters sneered at federal agents who urged them to settle down and grow corn. "I don't like corn," said Satanta. "It hurts my teeth." They also had no interest in raising cattle or standing in line for government rations. They wanted to follow ways of life based on the buffalo, just as their ancestors had. By the 1870s, however, hide hunters were slaughtering millions of

VOICE OF A PEOPLE

"Cheyenne, an ex-Marine, a member of the Cheyenne Dog Soldier Society." That is how contemporary Native American poet Lance Henson describes himself. For centuries, Native Americans have created songs, chants, and prayers to capture the spirit of their people. Today, Henson and many other Native American poets, including Kiowa N. Scott Momaday, are continuing this tradition. Henson lives in the 1990s. But the words to his poem "Warrior Nation Trilogy" might have been sung 200 years ago by his great-grandparents. The poem recalls a time when the plains belonged to the Cheyenne:

> we are the buffalo people
> we dwell in the light of our father sun
> in the shadow of our mother earth
> we are the beautiful people
> we roam the great plains without fear
> in our days the land has taught us oneness
> we alone breathe with the rivers
> we alone hear the song of the stones

buffalo a year. In 1874, a crisis developed when hide hunters appeared in the Texas Panhandle at a place called Adobe Walls (see map, page 49).

That spring, some Kiowa, including Satanta, vowed to wipe out the hide hunters. A Kiowa chief named Kicking Bird argued against it. He felt the raid would be a death sentence for the Kiowa. But Satanta and another leader, named Lone Wolf, refused to back down. Instead, they invited warriors from the Arapaho, the Cheyenne, the Kwahadi, and other Comanche bands to join them in a raid on Adobe Walls. About 700 agreed to take part. They also agreed that Quanah should act as leader.

On June 26, 1874, under the cover of darkness, the combined force crept up on the hide hunters. One hunter spotted them and shouted out a warning for the rest to take cover. There were only about 28 hunters, but they had telescopic sites on their high-powered rifles. From a great distance, they could pick off any Native American who dared show himself. After a daylong battle, the Native Americans fell back. They then vented their anger in raids on settlements throughout the area.

The outbreak of violence gave Sheridan an excuse to move against the Native Americans. Soon, columns of U.S. soldiers crisscrossed the lower plains. Some 4,000 Native Americans fled to the Texas Panhandle. There, a combined village of Kiowa, Cheyenne, and Comanche sought shelter at the heart of the last open buffalo range—in Palo Duro Canyon (see map, page 49).

Surrender Free of the reservation, the Native Americans celebrated the start of a new life. But their happiness was short-lived. The blazing summer sun cracked the earth and burned the grass. Then, autumn rains turned the canyon floor into a stream of mud. The worst disaster struck on September 28, 1874, when Colonel Ranald MacKenzie and his troops marched into the canyon.

MacKenzie let the warriors flee without a chase. He would let the plains winter finish the battle for him. MacKenzie set fire to the village and captured or killed nearly 1,500 Native American horses. When the first blizzards swept down, MacKenzie's troops moved back and forth across the plains, rounding up the near-frozen and starving Native Americans who had fled from Palo Duro. Leader after leader surrendered.

On June 2, 1875, an exhausted Quanah led the Kwahadi into Fort Sill. Over the next few years, a series of small, bitter fights took place between U.S. soldiers and other Native American groups. But the struggle for the southern plains was effectively over.

TAKING ANOTHER LOOK

1. What factors led to the destruction of the great buffalo herds of the plains?

2. Why did the battle of Palo Duro Canyon lead to the surrender of many groups of Native Americans?

3. *CRITICAL THINKING* Many Native Americans of the plains said that when the buffalo died, they died, too. Explain.

CHAPTER 4: CLOSE UP

1 Defeat of the Dog Soldiers

- The U.S. government hoped to bring peace to the southern plains through the signing of the Medicine Lodge Treaty in 1867 with the Arapaho, Kiowa, Comanche, Cheyenne, and Kiowa-Apache.
- Treaty violations led to renewed hostilities between the U.S. army and the Cheyenne in 1868.
- During a campaign in the winter of 1868–69, U.S. troops massacred Cheyenne residents of a village on Washita Creek. The campaign ended with most southern Cheyenne forced onto reservations.

2 War to Save the Buffalo

- Vast numbers of buffalo were slaughtered by professional and "sport" hunters, pushing the buffalo towards extinction.
- In 1874, Native American warriors led by Quanah attacked buffalo-hide hunters at Adobe Walls.
- Fleeing from U.S. soldiers, some 4,000 Native Americans settled in Palo Duro Canyon in Texas, only to be forced to flee again in late 1874.
- Most Native Americans in the southern Plains had surrendered to U.S. troops and were confined to reservations by 1875.

WHO, WHAT, WHERE

1. **Who** was Roman Nose?
2. **What** were Dog Soldiers?
3. **Where** was Medicine Lodge Creek?
4. **Who** was Black Kettle?
5. **Where** was the "Fight When Roman Nose Was Killed"?
6. **What** were Buffalo Soldiers?
7. **What** was the Washita Massacre?
8. **Who** was Quanah?
9. **Who** was Satanta?

UNDERSTANDING THE CHAPTER

1. What did the U.S. government and the Native American nations of the Great Plains agree to in the Medicine Lodge Treaty?

2. Why did Native Americans of the southern plains resist confinement to reservations?

3. How were the vast buffalo herds destroyed?

4. Why did Native Americans attack buffalo-hide hunters at Adobe Walls?

MAKING CONNECTIONS

1. What was the connection between the Sand Creek Massacre and the flight of the Cheyenne from General Hancock's troops in 1867?

2. What was the connection between the construction of the transcontinental railroads and the devastation of buffalo herds?

WRITING ABOUT HISTORY

1. Write a transcript of an oral history that a Dog Soldier might have told his family about the day that Roman Nose died.

2. Reporters from the eastern states attended the meeting at Medicine Lodge Creek. Write a newspaper article that describes this meeting and the treaty that was signed there.

3. Imagine you are Cynthia Ann Parker. Write a brief essay expressing your approval or disapproval of your son Quanah's attack at Adobe Walls.

4. The sight of hundreds of slaughtered buffalo provoked intense feelings of sorrow and anger in Native Americans of the plains. Write a short story in which you convey the reactions of a Native American family to this sight.

STRUGGLE FOR THE NORTHERN PLAINS

THINKING ABOUT THE CHAPTER

What events led to the loss of Native American homelands on the northern plains?

I n March 1930, Pretty Shield walked into the federal agency on the Crow reservation, between the Bighorn and Yellowstone rivers in Montana. A writer named Frank Linderman had asked her to come. Pretty Shield spoke to an interpreter rapidly in Crow. "She wants to know what it is that you wish her to tell you," explained the interpreter. Linderman replied, "About herself, everything that happened since she was a little girl." Hearing this, Pretty Shield laughed, "Ahhh! We shall be here until we die."

Linderman startled Pretty Shield by responding in sign language. "I want . . . a woman's story," signed Linderman, "a woman who has lived a long time." "Yes, Sign-talker," Pretty Shield replied, "I will tell you a woman's story—a woman's story about the Crow."

Day after day, the two talked in sign language. Pretty Shield's eyes sparkled when she recalled the former greatness of the Crow. She smiled as she told of buffalo hunts, her marriage to a horse soldier named Goes-Ahead, and the birth of her children.

One day Linderman brought up an unpleasant subject. He asked about events that led the Crow to

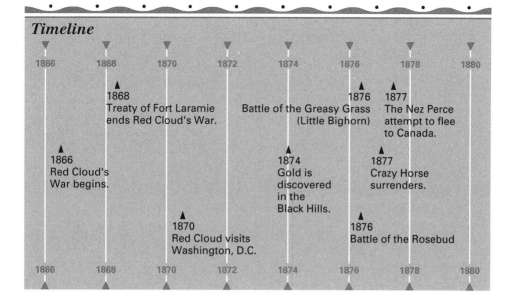

1866 1868 1870 1872 1874 1876 1878 1880

▲ 1868
Treaty of Fort Laramie
ends Red Cloud's War.

▲ 1876
Battle of the Greasy Grass
(Little Bighorn)

▲ 1877
The Nez Perce
attempt to flee
to Canada.

▲ 1866
Red Cloud's
War begins.

▲ 1874
Gold is
discovered
in the
Black Hills.

▲ 1877
Crazy Horse
surrenders.

▲ 1870
Red Cloud visits
Washington, D.C.

▲ 1876
Battle of the Rosebud

1866 1868 1870 1872 1874 1876 1878 1880

the reservation. Pretty Shield covered her face as painful memories flooded back—the destruction of the buffalo, the death of a daughter, and the loss of the Crow homelands. "Our men fought hard against our enemies," she said, "but with everything going wrong, we began to be whipped."

This chapter explores the final efforts by Native Americans on the northern plains to hold back the press of settlers from the east. When those efforts ended in defeat, said Pretty Shield, "our old ways seemed like a dream."

1 RED CLOUD'S WAR

How did Red Cloud lead the Lakota to a victory over U.S. troops on the northern plains?

In 1866, a scout ran through an Oglala village shouting, "The *Wasichus* are coming!" Still only a child, Black Elk had never seen a *Wasichu*, the name given to white people. He asked his grandfather, "What does it mean?"

Black Elk's grandfather told him about a yellow metal that made the *Wasichus* crazy. They had found much of it in the mountains in the western part of what is now the state of Montana.

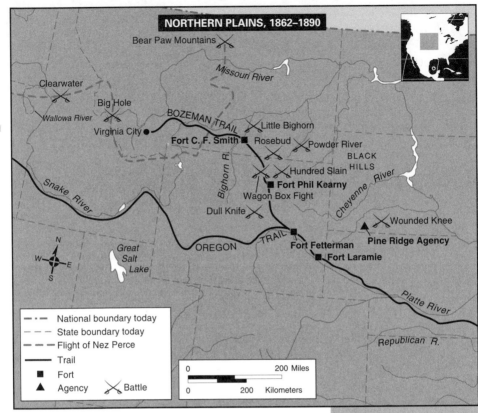

NORTHERN PLAINS, 1862–1890

Bear Paw Mountains
Missouri River
Clearwater
Big Hole
Wallowa River
BOZEMAN TRAIL
Virginia City
Little Bighorn
Fort C. F. Smith
Rosebud
Powder River
BLACK HILLS
Bighorn R.
Hundred Slain
Fort Phil Kearny
Cheyenne River
Wagon Box Fight
Snake River
Dull Knife
Wounded Knee
Pine Ridge Agency
N
W E
S
Great Salt Lake
OREGON TRAIL
Fort Fetterman
Fort Laramie
Platte River
Republican R.

National boundary today
State boundary today
Flight of Nez Perce
Trail
Fort
Agency
Battle

0   200 Miles
0 200 Kilometers

What battles took place on or near the Bozeman Trail? About how far is it from the Bear Paw Mountains to the U.S.-Canada border?

Stopping the Bozeman Trail Other Lakota peoples were angered by the intruders, too, and attacked road-building parties on their land. U.S. government officials saw the road as a vital link between Fort Laramie and both the Montana gold mines and the Oregon Trail (see map). In June 1866, federal officials invited Lakota leaders to a meeting at Fort Laramie to talk about the road, which they called the Bozeman Trail. The group included leaders of subgroups of the Lakota, among them Sitting Bull of the Hunkpapa, Spotted Tail of the Brulé, and Red Cloud of the Oglala.

The officials asked the Lakota to give up "land no wider than a wagon wheel" for the road. In exchange, they offered payments of goods and a promise not to disturb the animals the Native Americans hunted. On June 13, the rattling and creaking of wagons interrupted the talks as 700 U.S. soldiers arrived at the fort. Building supplies filled their wagons. The party's leader, Colonel Henry Carrington, made no secret of his purpose. He had come to build forts on the Bozeman Trail.

Red Cloud protested strongly. "[The U.S. President] sends us presents and wants us to sell him the road. But the White Chief [Carrington] goes with soldiers to steal the road before . . . [we] say yes or no!" Red Cloud walked out, and most Lakota leaders followed.

Battle of the Hundred Slain Colonel Carrington marched into Lakota territory confident of the fighting abilities of his soldiers, most of them Civil War veterans. The hardened troops scoffed at the fighting abilities of Native Americans. "Give me eighty men and I would ride through the whole Sioux [Lakota] nation," boasted one soldier, Captain William Fetterman. But the U.S. troops had no experience in the Native American style of warfare.

All along the road, Native Americans made hit-and-run raids on the soldiers. Still, Carrington managed to reinforce Fort Reno. He also built two new posts on the Bozeman Trail, Fort Phil Kearny and Fort C. F. Smith (see map).

In "the Moon of the Popping Trees" (December) 1866, the Lakota decided to focus their efforts on Fort Phil Kearny, Carrington's headquarters. They settled on a bold plan devised by Crazy Horse. First, a band of Lakota fell upon a group of soldiers gathering wood outside the fort. As expected, when Carrington heard the gunfire, he sent out reinforcements, 79 men under the command of Captain Fetterman.

As Fetterman headed out, Crazy Horse and the Lakota pretended to retreat. Fetterman took the bait and chased after them. The Lakota led the bluecoats on a wild chase, out of sight of the fort, toward hundreds of Lakota, lying hidden in gullies off the trail. When the U.S. troops charged past, the Lakota launched their attack.

In the fighting that followed, the Lakota wiped out Fetterman and his soldiers. Non-Native Americans called the battle a massacre. The Lakota called it the Battle of the Hundred Slain, after the number of U.S. troops the Lakota believed they had killed.

Pushing Out the *Wasichus* The victory spurred Red Cloud to step up his attacks. Joining him were the northern

Cheyenne, led by Dull Knife and Little Wolf. By their raids on railroads and wagon trains, the Cheyenne and Lakota all but stopped travel across the northern plains.

The federal government responded by sending in more troops, armed with new rapid-firing rifles. In August 1867, Army officers claimed victories over the Cheyenne at the Hayfield Fight near Fort C. F. Smith and the Lakota in the Wagon Box Fight at Fort Phil Kearny. But neither battle stopped Native American raids on the northern plains. The government then decided to pursue a policy of peace—for the moment. In May 1868, the Fort Laramie Treaty ended the

Native American leaders Sitting Bull, Swift Bear, Spotted Tail, and Red Cloud (front row, left to right) were photographed in the 1880's after the end of the Plains wars.

fighting on Red Cloud's terms. U.S. troops were removed from forts along the Bozeman Trail, and Red Cloud then agreed to stop his raids. After the U.S. troops had marched away, the Lakota burned the forts to the ground.

Visit to Washington In 1868, Red Cloud boasted, "I have more soldiers than the Great Father [President], and he cannot take my lands against my will." But Red Cloud soon learned otherwise. In 1870, he went to visit President Ulysses S. Grant to ask for an end to violations of the Fort Laramie Treaty. On May 26, Red Cloud and 15 other Oglala leaders boarded a train that would carry them to Washington, D.C.

Federal officials escorted Red Cloud around the capital, attempting to impress him with the might of the United States. For example, they showed off a cannon so big that a soldier could crawl into its barrel. But Red Cloud refused to let such displays of power overwhelm him. When officials pressed him to accept a reservation along the Missouri River, Red Cloud held out for a site in the Oglala homeland along the Platte River.

When Red Cloud went home, he carried an agreement that set up a temporary federal agency in the Oglala homeland. But he also carried sorrow in his heart. His visit had convinced Red Cloud that the Lakota could not resist the non-Native Americans forever. He never went to war again. Instead, Red Cloud traveled a total of seven times to Washington, D.C., to fight through his words for his people's rights. Other Lakota, however, vowed to fight as they always had—from horseback.

TAKING ANOTHER LOOK

1. Why did Red Cloud declare war against the non-Native Americans?

2. How did Red Cloud's visit to Washington, D.C., change his attitude toward resistance?

3. *CRITICAL THINKING* What arguments do you think Red Cloud would have used with federal officials in Washington when arguing for remaining in the Lakota homeland, near the Platte River?

2 SCATTERING OF THE PEOPLE
What final battles were waged by Native Americans on the northern plains?

The Fort Laramie Treaty of 1868 had created a huge reservation for the Lakota in the Dakota Territory. In addition, the lands west of the reservation were known as "unceded Indian territory," lands that Native Americans had not given up in treaties. Here, Native Americans were free to travel, hunt, and live. Yet by the early 1870s, both the reservation and the unceded lands were being threatened.

In "the Moon of the Red Cherries" (July) 1874, Lakota scouts spotted U.S. soldiers prowling the *Paha Sapa*, the Black Hills. The Fort Laramie Treaty barred *Wasichus* from entering the hills, an area the Lakota considered sacred. But George Armstrong Custer (see page 47), now assigned to the northern plains, paid no heed to the treaty. Instead, his soldiers searched for the yellow metal. They found it, too, and Custer announced that the Black Hills were filled with gold "from the grass roots down."

Not for Lease or Sale By 1875, gold-hungry prospectors were swarming into the Black Hills. Red Cloud and Spotted Tail protested the treaty violation to federal officials. In response, the government sent commissioners to lease or buy the Black Hills from the Native Americans.

When the meeting opened, the nervous commissioners stared out at a sea of people. So important were the Black Hills that thousands of Lakota, Cheyenne, and Arapaho had come. Followers of Crazy Horse arrived dressed for war. One horse soldier danced his horse up to the commissioners and warned, "I will kill the first chief who speaks for selling the Black Hills!" The Native Americans refused to sell or lease the Black Hills for any price.

Preparing for War The badly shaken commissioners returned home seething with anger. Their report led the government to order all Native Americans onto reservations. Any who refused would be considered hostile and subject to war.

Pretty Shield was photographed in the 1930s. Her husband, Goes-Ahead, served as one of the Army's Crow scouts during the 1876 campaign on the plains

The government quickly prepared to act. With the defeat of most Native American nations on the southern plains, U.S. troops were freed to move north. Government officials also attempted to convince nations that were traditional enemies of the Lakota to join with the U.S. Army against the Lakota. Anger at the destruction of the buffalo herds caused some groups to resist. But the Crow finally agreed to help the federal government. "When the war is over," explained Chief Plenty Coups, "the soldier-chiefs will not forget that the Crows came to their aid."

The Cheyenne and Lakota braced for war early in 1876. The first battle came in March, when General George Crook marched into the Powder River valley. There, his troops launched a surprise attack on a peaceful hunting village and set its tipis ablaze. When Sitting Bull learned of the incident, he declared: "These soldiers have come shooting; they want war. All right, we'll give it to them!" He called for Lakota, Cheyenne, and Arapaho to gather at a site along Rosebud Creek in Montana Territory.

Battle Where the Girl Saved Her Brother Thousands of Native Americans joined Sitting Bull and Crazy Horse. Oglala and Brulé who had fled the reservation warned that three columns of U.S. soldiers were headed toward the Native American encampment. The first column to arrive was led by "Three Stars," the name given to Crook. On June 17, 1876, Crazy Horse and Sitting Bull led about 1,300 warriors in an attack on Crook's column of about the same number.

The battle raged for six hours. The brilliant riding skills and the courage of the Native Americans created chaos among Crook's cavalry. Crazy Horse, for example, rode headlong at the rapidly firing troops, reared up his horse, and sped off. Then he turned, and rushed the soldiers again. Other Lakota followed his example.

The Cheyenne also showed off their war skills. In one dangerous charge, Chief Comes-in-Sight had his horse shot out from under him close to the U.S. troops. He had begun to sing his death song when another rider swerved between him and the soldiers. In a flash, he jumped on the rider's horse. The rider turned out to be his sister, Buffalo-Calf-Road-Woman.

The Cheyenne remembered the fight as the Battle Where the Girl Saved Her Brother. The U.S. Army called it the

In the 1880s, a Cheyenne artist, who had taken part in the battle at the Greasy Grass, painted this view of Custer's defeat.

Battle of the Rosebud. By any name, it was a Native American victory. By sunset, Crook was in retreat.

Along the Greasy Grass The Lakota and Cheyenne moved to a meadow along the Greasy Grass River, known to non-Native Americans as the Little Bighorn. Here, they danced and feasted to celebrate their victory. Unaware of Crook's defeat, meanwhile, the other columns of U.S. troops marched on. Acting on a tip from a scout, they headed toward the Greasy Grass. General Alfred Terry and Colonel John Gibbon marched to the northern end of the river. Colonel Custer split off from Terry's forces and marched toward the southern end with about 600 men.

On June 25, 1876, Custer reached the Greasy Grass. Up to 15,000 Native Americans, from as far away as Canada, had responded to Sitting Bull's call for help. Their tipis stretched some 3 miles [5 kilometers] along the banks of the river. Unaccountably, Custer decided to attack rather than wait for Terry and Gibbon. He split his troops, sending some to each end of the village.

Unaware of the approach of the U.S. troops, Native American women dug turnips at the river's edge. A group of boys, including 13-year-old Black Elk, splashed in the water. A lookout, spotting Custer's troops, shattered the calm: "The chargers are coming! They are charging!"

The Greasy Grass valley filled with dust and gun smoke. Custer, a brave and sometimes reckless fighter, was overmatched. His soldiers faced the greatest Native American war chiefs of the time—Crazy Horse, Sitting Bull, Gall, Two Moon, and more. The Hunkpapa nearly wiped out the soldiers who attacked the southern edge of the village, forcing the survivors to flee to a defensive position cut off from Custer and the rest of his troops.

Native Americans now fell upon Custer with full force. They took no prisoners. "We were fighting for our lives and our homelands," declared Joseph White Bull. When the dust cleared, the bodies of 215 U.S. soldiers lay scattered on a hill above the Greasy Grass, Custer's among them.

Surrender As telegraphs and newspapers spread the shocking news of Custer's defeat across the United States, the government renewed its efforts to punish the Native

THE UNENDING BATTLE

To this day, people argue over events and decisions in the battle fought by Native Americans and Custer's troops at the Greasy Grass. The battle site has been preserved as a historic monument. Each year, thousands of tourists visit, seeking to understand what happened there.

Generations of non-Native Americans grew up with the image of gallant U.S. troops making a heroic last stand—an image encouraged by a government that wanted to seize Native American lands. Until recently, most ignored Native American testimony that suggested a less heroic fight. Then, in 1989, archaeologists uncovered evidence indicating that U.S. troops may have panicked. But some Native American testimony from the period claims that Custer's men fought bravely. Could Native Americans have said this to escape the wrath of federal officials?

In 1991, Custer lost a second battle, this time in the U.S. Congress. In December of that year, the House of Representatives removed his name from the historic battlefield. To honor all the participants in the battle—U.S. troops and Native Americans, they changed the name of the site from Custer Battlefield to Little Bighorn National Monument.

Americans who had won the victory. Government officials redrew the boundaries of the Lakota reservation, taking away about a third of its land, including the Black Hills. Meanwhile, U.S. troops relentlessly tracked the Cheyenne and Lakota across the northern plains.

Sitting Bull and Gall led their people north into Canada, but Native Americans who remained in the United States remained under constant pressure from U.S. troops. As food grew short and casualties mounted, nation after nation was forced onto reservation lands. Black Elk called it the "scattering of the people." Even the Crow, who had aided the government, did not escape resettlement.

In May 1877, Crazy Horse marched onto a reservation with some 800 horse soldiers dressed for war. They had come not to fight, however, but to surrender and accept life on the reservation. Four months later, Crazy Horse was dead, killed by a U.S. soldier with a bayonet.

The battle for the northern plains was over. In 1881, Sitting Bull led his homesick people back to the United States and onto a reservation. By then, the buffalo had nearly disappeared. Huge fenced-in ranches had replaced the herds. "We could not travel," said Pretty Shield sadly. "But there was little good in traveling. There was nothing left to travel for."

TAKING ANOTHER LOOK

1. What had the Lakota been promised by the Fort Laramie Treaty?
2. Why did government policy change toward Native Americans on the northern plains after 1874?
3. *CRITICAL THINKING* What did Pretty Shield mean by her statement "There was nothing left to travel for"?

3 FLIGHT OF THE NEZ PERCE
Why did the Nez Perce try to flee to Canada?

The war for the northern plains had ended with Crazy Horse's surrender. But that same year, U.S. troops and Native Americans again fought there. This time, however, the Native Americans were not people of the plains. They were Nez Perce, fleeing east from their homeland in the Wallowa Valley of Oregon in an attempt to remain free.

Land Grabbers For many years, settlers moving west had shown little interest in the cool Wallowa Valley. But in the 1870s, they realized that the lands were ideal for grazing. Soon non-Native Americans pressured the federal government to open the region to settlement.

In 1877, the government assigned General Oliver O. Howard to force the Nez Perce from the Wallowa Valley, claiming they had sold the lands under an earlier treaty.

Howard talked to Nez Perce Chief Heinmot Tooyaleet, also known as Joseph.

Joseph refused to give up the land, and Howard threw him in jail. Howard then reminded Joseph of the fate of Native Americans on the plains and gave the Nez Perce 30 days to get out of the Wallowa Valley and onto a reservation in Idaho.

Chief Joseph felt it was suicide to fight. After his release from jail, he counseled his people, "Better to live in peace than to begin a war and lay dead." As the Nez Perce began the overland march, several embittered Native American youths killed four settlers. Other young warriors also struck out in anger, raiding and killing.

On July 11, General Howard vowed to teach the Nez Perce a lesson. He cornered them on the south fork of the Clearwater River in Idaho Territory. Although outnumbered six to one, Nez Perce fighters held off the troops and gave the women and children a chance to escape.

This photograph of Chief Joseph and his family was taken in 1890. Until his death in 1904, Joseph urged the U.S. government to return Nez Perce lands in the Wallowa Valley.

Prairie Trek Nez Perce leaders now met to decide what to do next. They convinced Joseph to lead the Nez Perce across the Rocky Mountains to the northern plains, where they believed they could hunt buffalo and be safe among other Native American peoples. Thus began an amazing 1,700-mile [2,700-kilometer] trek that captured the nation's attention (see map, page 62).

For nearly three months, Joseph led some 800 people across rugged mountains and rolling grasslands. The group included 300 warriors and 500 women, children, and old people. General Howard kept close behind with some 600 troops. But time and again, the Nez Perce eluded capture. When pursuers and pursued clashed, the Nez Perce, armed with old guns, managed to outfight the soldiers.

By early October, the Nez Perce were within 30 miles [50 kilometers] of the Canadian border. Then, a force led by General Howard and General Nelson Miles, with another 600 soldiers, surrounded them near the Bear Paw Mountains in Montana. The troops came armed with cannons and machine guns. Still, the Nez Perce held out. But many Nez Perce had been killed during their long flight, and only 80 warriors and 350 women and children remained. Food was in short supply, and the first snows of the harsh prairie winter had fallen. The time had come to surrender.

On October 5, 1877, Chief Joseph rode across the field alone. He then faced General Howard. Through a translator he said, "From where the sun now stands I will fight no more forever." With these words, the history of a free Nez Perce people closed. The army never allowed Chief Joseph to return to the Wallowa Valley. In 1904, he died on the Colville reservation in Washington. The reservation doctor reported the cause of death as "a broken heart."

TAKING ANOTHER LOOK

1. Why were the Nez Perce forced off their lands in the Wallowa Valley?

2. What did the Nez Perce hope to accomplish by fleeing east?

3. *CRITICAL THINKING* How did the flight of the Nez Perce symbolize the fate of Native Americans by the late 1800s?

KEY IDEAS

1 Red Cloud's War

- In 1866, the federal goverment began to build forts along the Bozeman Trail. This provoked the Lakota leader Red Cloud to declare war.
- In May 1868, the Fort Laramie Treaty ended the fighting on Red Cloud's terms by closing down the forts along the Bozeman Trail.

2 Scattering of the People

- In the 1870s, gold-hungry prospectors violated the Fort Laramie Treaty by entering the Black Hills. Native Americans refused to give up their land without a fight.
- In 1876, the Lakota, Cheyenne, and Arapaho won victories over U.S. troops in battles on the Rosebud and Greasy Grass (Little Bighorn) rivers.
- The U.S. government sent more troops to the plains. By 1877, fighting was over and Native Americans were confined to reservations.

3 Flight of the Nez Perce

- The Nez Perce were ordered from their homeland in the Wallowa Valley in Oregon to a reservation in 1877.
- Joseph and other Nez Perce leaders decided to flee to the northern plains, clashing with U.S. troops many times during the flight.
- In October 1887, faced with winter, little food, and heavy casualties, Joseph surrendered and the Nez Perce were confined to a reservation.

WHO, WHAT, WHERE

1. **Who** were the *Wasichus*?
2. **Who** was Spotted Tail?
3. **Who** was Red Cloud?
4. **Where** were Fort C. F. Smith and Fort Phil Kearny located?
5. **Where** are the *Paha Sapa*?
6. **Who** was Crazy Horse?

7. **What** was the "Battle Where the Girl Saved Her Brother"?

8. **Who** was Heinmot Tooyaleet?

9. **Where** did U.S. troops surround the Nez Perce?

UNDERSTANDING THE CHAPTER

1. Why did Red Cloud and other Native Americans want to close down the Bozeman Trail?

2. How did non-Native Americans violate the Fort Laramie Treaty in the early 1870s?

3. How did the U.S. government respond to Custer's defeat at Greasy Grass River?

4. Why did Joseph and other Nez Perce leaders attempt to flee to the northern plains?

MAKING CONNECTIONS

1. What was the connection between Red Cloud's visit to Washington, D.C., and his change of tactics in fighting for Lakota rights?

2. What was the connection between the defeat of the Native American nations in the southern plains and the war on the northern plains in 1876?

3. What was the connection between the destruction of the buffalo and the eventual confinement of Native Americans of the plains on reservations?

WRITING ABOUT HISTORY

1. In 1875, Red Cloud protested violations of the Fort Laramie Treaty to federal officials. Write a letter Red Cloud could have sent to the U.S. President.

2. If you had been a Crow leader in 1876, how would you have responded to a request from U.S. Army officials to join their campaign against the Lakota? Write your reply in the form of a speech.

3. Imagine you are a Nez Perce leader in 1877. Write a speech to convince Joseph to flee to the northern plains instead of going to the reservation in Idaho.

CHAPTER 6

DEATH OF A DREAM

THINKING ABOUT THE CHAPTER

What hardships awaited Native Americans once they resettled on the reservations?

SECTIONS

1 The Broken Hoop

2 Uprooting a Heritage

3 Ghost Dancers

I n August 1877, U.S. soldiers marched the Northern Cheyenne onto a parched reservation in Indian Territory. There, hunger and disease took a terrible toll on the Northern Cheyenne. Dull Knife and Little Wolf watched in horror as their people dwindled from almost 1,000 to fewer than 300. In July 1878, the two leaders pleaded with a federal agent to allow the Northern Cheyenne to return to their homelands. "We cannot stay another year," declared Little Wolf, "we may all be dead."

When the agent refused their request, Dull Knife and Little Wolf planned a breakout. In September, 297 Cheyenne began a desperate trip north. Some 13,000 soldiers and civilians soon joined in a hunt for the Northern Cheyenne. But the Northern Cheyenne managed to make it across the Platte River, where the group split up.

In October, soldiers caught up with Dull Knife's band in Nebraska. They imprisoned the Native Americans, but Dull Knife organized another breakout, in which about 30 Cheyenne were killed. The final, bloody roundup of Dull Knife's band came 12 days later.

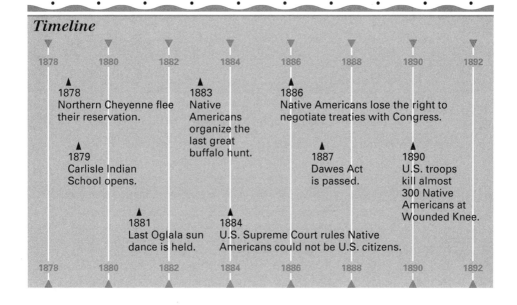

1878
1880
1882
1884
1886
1888
1890
1892

1878
Northern Cheyenne flee
their reservation.

1883
Native
Americans
organize the
last great
buffalo hunt.

1886
Native Americans lose the right to
negotiate treaties with Congress.

1879
Carlisle Indian
School opens.

1887
Dawes Act
is passed.

1890
U.S. troops
kill almost
300 Native
Americans at
Wounded Knee.

1881
Last Oglala sun
dance is held.

1884
U.S. Supreme Court rules Native
Americans could not be U.S. citizens.

1878
1880
1882
1884
1886
1888
1890
1892

Little Wolf's Cheyenne had wintered in Nebraska. By March 1879, these battered Northern Cheyenne, now numbering only about 80, made their way into Montana Territory, where U.S. troops cornered them. The government then changed its policy. It allowed these Cheyenne to settle on the Pine Ridge Reservation with the Lakota and, later, to move to a reservation in an area of Montana, which had been their home. This chapter tells of Native American adjustment—and resistance—to reservation life.

1 THE BROKEN HOOP

How did reservation life force Native Americans to abandon many old ways?

In September 1883, Lakota scouts rushed to a reservation in Montana Territory with important news. They had spotted a huge herd of buffalo at the Tongue River. Better yet, federal officials had granted them a permit to organize a hunt. This was the last great buffalo hunt on the plains. A white rancher who rode with the Lakota captured six live buffalo to raise on his ranch. Soon, buffalo were so rare that tourists visited the ranch to see them.

As the plains filled with settlers, other game dwindled, too. Any Native American who dared to escape from a reservation could no longer rely on traditional sources of food. The lives of Native Americans were now tied to the reservations.

Ration Lines and Hoes Native Americans on reservations lined up to collect tickets for **rations,** or set amounts of goods, provided by the government. On issue days, they turned in the tickets for food, clothing, and other goods, such as farming tools, promised in the treaties. Native Americans especially looked forward to issue days when federal agents distributed cattle.

After federal agents stamped the ration tickets, Native American hunters stampeded the cattle across the prairie. Then they chased after the cattle, firing arrows from horseback. "Issue days were big times for all of us," recalled Arapaho artist Carl Sweezy. "For a few hours, the Arapaho once more knew some of the excitement of the old buffalo hunt." But federal agents wanted to put an end to traditional Native American practices. So they ordered that the cattle be slaughtered before being shipped to reservations.

This 1882 engraving shows a group of Plains Native Americans exchanging ration tickets for supplies at a store on their reservation.

Issue days lost their joy. Federal agents told Native Americans they must learn to farm. Government rations, they warned, would not last forever. But the lands given to Native Americans for reservations often were not suitable for farming because of poor soil and inadequate rainfall.

Vanishing Ways One after another, traditional practices vanished or were greatly altered. Instead of buffalo skins, Native Americans now covered their tipis with government-issued canvas. They gathered the tipis into camps and tried to live as they had when they were free to travel the plains. But federal agents pressured them into building one-room log cabins on separate tracts of land.

Supplies of materials for many traditional crafts practiced by women also ended when the buffalo hunts did. Instead of working with soft buffalo skins, women made do with cattle hides or preprocessed leather to fashion footgear, belts, or new items such as ration-ticket pouches. They now decorated clothing with glass beads rather than hand-tooled bone beads.

Native American men also struggled to keep old ways alive. Some fled the reservations to make raids on traditional enemies. The Blackfeet stole horses from the Crow. The Crow stole them back. At other times, hunters prowled old hunting grounds looking for game. But they rarely shot more than a few rabbits.

Federal agents cracked down on roving warriors by hiring Native American police officers to patrol the reservations. This practice pitted Native American against Native American. It also gave agents a way to bypass the traditional power of chiefs. The shift in power left Native Americans bewildered. "We knew no other way but to listen to our chiefs," explained Pretty Shield.

Ending the Sun Dances Despair deepened in the 1880s, when federal officials banned Native American **sun dances**. Some 20 nations held these religious ceremonies each fall or spring to ensure earth's continued bounty. Native Americans danced for days, praying for visions that would give them spiritual guidance. To strengthen their prayers, dancers suspended themselves from a pole by rawhide ropes attached to wooden skewers beneath their skin.

The sun dances disturbed non-Native Americans who failed to understand their spiritual meaning. When federal agents outlawed the sun dances, a member of the Blackfeet voiced his fears: "If they deprive us of our religions, we will have nothing left!"

Black Elk, who remembered the great vision he had had as a child, painted a bleak picture of the Pine Ridge Reservation in 1883. He lamented:

> All our people were now settling in square gray houses, scattered here and there across this hungry land, and around them the *Wasichus* had drawn a line to keep them in. The nation's sacred hoop was broken, and there was no center any longer for the holy tree. . . . I felt like crying.

TAKING ANOTHER LOOK

1. How did Native Americans try to cling to old ways?
2. How did agency officials force them to abandon many of these practices?
3. *CRITICAL THINKING* Why do you think use of Native American police weakened the power of the chiefs?

2 UPROOTING A HERITAGE

What policies and laws in the late 1800s threatened Native American cultures?

In the summer of 1884, "Buffalo Bill" Cody, a former buffalo hunter and army scout, visited the Standing Rock Reservation in what is now North Dakota. Cody wanted permission to take Sitting Bull on tour with his Wild West Show. The federal agent welcomed the chance to get the popular Hunkpapa chief off the reservation, since Sitting Bull remained a symbol of resistance. He stubbornly defied efforts to force Native Americans to accept new ways.

For two years, Sitting Bull visited major cities throughout the United States and Canada. Members of other Plains nations accompanied the show, too. They performed the dances and songs of their people to the applause of audiences everywhere. Sitting Bull thought it odd that so many whites would pay money to see the cultures they sought to destroy. In 1887, Cody asked Sitting Bull to tour Europe. But Sitting Bull declined the offer. "I am needed here," he explained. He then returned to the agency to resist a new federal policy toward Native Americans.

Learning Other Ways In the late 1800s, reformers felt the best way to help Native Americans was by teaching them the "American" way of life. These reformers showed little interest in preserving Native American culture. Instead, they sought to break the cultural ties that bound the Native American nations together. They wanted to **Americanize** Native Americans, or make them accept the ways of white U.S. society. Once Native Americans had been Americanized, reservations could be eliminated entirely.

Native American leaders such as Sitting Bull and Crazy Horse protested Americanization. "We do not want your civilization!" said Crazy Horse. "We would live as our fathers did, and their fathers before them." Yet, by 1877, most Native Americans on the plains and elsewhere had been confined to reservations, where agents worked to stamp out old ways of life. "We are prisoners of war," said Black Elk. "Our power is gone, and we are dying [as a people.]"

These Apache children were photographed in March 1887, just four months after their arrival at the Carlisle School in Pennsylvania.

While agents pressured adults to abandon old traditions, reformers sent Native American children off to school. The Cherokee clung to their children—and their culture—by building their own schools. "Remember that the whites are near us," advised one Cherokee leader. "Unless you can speak their language, read and write as they do, they will . . . trample on your rights." On most reservations, however, parents had little say in the education of their children. Reformers often separated Native American children from their parents and shipped them off to boarding schools.

Living in Two Worlds Some boarding schools lay within walking distance of the reservation. Others lay halfway across the continent in the eastern states. At the boarding schools, teachers stressed the superiority of non-Native American ways. "I believe in immersing the Indians in our civilization," stated the founder of Pennsylvania's Carlisle Indian Industrial School. "Immersing the Indians" meant making them give up everything that looked or sounded Native American. Recalled Carl Sweezy, "We had to learn to cut our hair short, and to wear close-fitting clothes made of dull-colored cloth, . . . even though we knew that our long braids of hair and embroidered robes . . . were more beautiful."

At the schools, Native Americans learned to pledge allegiance to the U.S. flag and to celebrate Thanksgiving and Independence Day. Boys were taught to fix fences, plant crops, and milk cows. Girls were taught to cook unfamiliar foods and make dresses. "Don't look back," warned one teacher at Carlisle. "All that you knew is passed away."

When children returned from the boarding schools, they felt like strangers. Some tore off tightly buttoned clothes and put on the traditional clothing of their people. But the children now knew the ways of two widely different worlds. The experience often left them torn and confused.

Legal Ground Lost While reformers robbed Native Americans of their cultures, the government limited their legal rights. In 1871, Congress passed a law ending treaty-making with Native American nations. Laws could then be passed by Congress without asking Native Americans to sign agreements. In 1884, the Supreme Court denied citizenship to Native Americans. (Congress did not confer citizenship on Native Americans until 1924.) In 1886, the Supreme Court extended the right of Congress to exercise its authority over Native Americans as it saw fit by declaring them "**wards** of the United States," or communties dependent on the federal government.

To further weaken Native American nations, Congress moved to divide up the reservations. In 1887, it passed the General Allotment Act, also known as the **Dawes Act**. Under it, heads of Native American families were each to select a 160-acre [64-hectare] plot of land on their reservation; they received additional land based on the size of their families. If the head of a family refused to pick a plot, the government would assign one. To protect the plots from greedy land speculators, Native American owners were barred from selling them for 25 years. Any reservation lands not distributed to Native Americans could be sold or leased by the federal government to non-Native American settlers.

Native Americans such as Sitting Bull furiously protested the Dawes Act as a land-grab. The evidence shows the protesters were correct. Between 1887 and 1934, when a new law overturned the Dawes Act, Native American land holdings shrank from 138 million acres [55 million hectares] to 55 million acres [22 million hectares].

TAKING ANOTHER LOOK

1. What did reformers hope to accomplish by starting boarding schools for Native American children?
2. How did the Dawes Act affect Native Americans?
3. *CRITICAL THINKING* Reformers called themselves "friends of the Indians." How might Sitting Bull reply to that description? Explain.

3 GHOST DANCERS

How did the Ghost Dance demonstrate the longing of Native Americans for their lost heritage?

In the late 1880s, delegations of Native Americans from all over the Great Plains made their way west to Nevada. Word had spread that a Paiute prophet there named Wovoka (WOH-voh-kah) had received a new vision offering hope to Native Americans.

The visitors sat spellbound as Wovoka described his vision. Wovoka taught them sacred songs and a special dance revealed to him in the vision. He warned them to live good lives and to prepare for the coming of God.

A Cheyenne named Kicking Bear helped spread the teachings of Wovoka across the plains. He spoke to the Hunkpapa at their reservation in South Dakota, repeating the message that Wovoka had received from God:

> The earth is getting old, and I will make it new
> for my chosen people, the Indians. . . . I will cov-
> er the earth with new soil, . . . and under this soil
> will be buried the whites. . . . The new lands will
> be covered with sweet-grass and running water
> and trees, and herds of buffalo and ponies will
> stray over it, so that my . . . children [the Indians]
> may eat and drink, hunt and rejoice.

Kicking Bear then taught the Hunkpapa what became known as the **Ghost Dance**—a dance that would unite Native Americans with the spirits of their ancestors.

Wovoka preached his message at a time when severe food shortages and widespread epidemics were weakening Plains Native Americans. These peoples were already disheartened by confinement on reservations. Amid hunger and sickness, the Ghost Dance held out a ray of hope. It spread like wildfire among the Plains peoples.

Death of Sitting Bull Wovoka preached, "You must not hurt anybody or do harm to anyone." But Sitting Bull still worried that the sight of Ghost Dancers would bring soldiers onto the reservation. When he expressed these fears, Kicking Bear replied that if the dancers wore sacred shirts—Ghost Shirts with magic markings—no harm would come to them. Even bullets could not pierce the shirts.

Talk of the Ghost Shirts convinced federal officials that the dances were war dances. Some 3,000 U.S. troops were quickly sent to the Lakota reservations. The arrival of the troops spread panic among the Na-

This photograph of a group of Lakota Ghost Dancers was taken late in 1890, shortly before the massacre at Wounded Knee.

A LASTING MONUMENT

Wounded Knee has remained a lasting symbol of the injustices suffered by Native Americans at the hands of the federal government. In 1973, members of a Native American rights group called the American Indian Movement (AIM) took over buildings at Wounded Knee on the Pine Ridge Reservation. They occupied the area for 71 days, calling for the right of Native Americans to run their own affairs. Gunfire erupted once again as federal marshals moved in to end the seige. As part of their defense in the trials that followed, AIM leaders focused on the trail of broken treaties that had led them to occupy the buildings at Wounded Knee. In the end, the federal government failed to win any convictions.

Today, a simple stone shaft marks the mass grave where hundreds of Native Americans lost their lives in 1890. On three sides of the shaft are listed the names of those buried at the site. The long, narrow grave is a powerful reminder of the words spoken by Black Elk: "A people's dream died here."

tive Americans and many fled the reservation to camps in the Badlands of South Dakota.

Federal officials decided to crack down on those they believed were leaders of the Ghost Dance among the Lakota. One of these was Sitting Bull. Officials at the Standing Rock Agency ordered his arrest. On December 15, 1890, Ghost Dancers tried to prevent Native American police from carrying out the arrest. In the fighting that followed, Sitting Bull was shot and killed.

Wounded Knee With Sitting Bull dead, the next target for arrest was Big Foot, a leader of the Miniconjou (mihn-UH-kahn-joo) band of the Lakota. On December 28, 1890, soldiers caught up with Big Foot as he led some 350 Miniconjou, including 230 women and children, toward Pine Ridge. Big Foot, badly weakened by pneumonia, offered no resistance. Soldiers ordered the band to set up camp alongside the Wounded Knee Creek.

Early the next morning, soldiers moved through the camp collecting weapons. When a Native American named Black Coyote failed to lay down his gun, a soldier tried to take it. In the struggle, the rifle went off. At the sound of the shot, U.S. troops opened fire with rifles and cannons. "We tried to run," recalled Louise Weasel Bear, "but they shot us like we were buffalo." Nearly all Native Americans at the camp were killed.

The Last Battle The sound of gunfire reached other Native Americans on the reservation, almost 20 miles away. Several Lakota, including Black Elk, leapt onto their horses. When they reached Wounded Knee, they saw bodies strewn on the ground and attacked U.S. troops rounding up the wounded. The Lakota killed two before taking off to camps in the Badlands where the Ghost Dancers had fled.

Some Lakota leaders called for war. But in the end, Red Cloud convinced his people to leave the Badlands and return to the reservation. To do otherwise would mean yet more death. Group after group complied. "And so it was all over," said Black Elk.

On New Year's Day 1891, a group of soldiers and Native Americans buried the victims at Wounded Knee. As they covered a huge mass grave, a blizzard hit. Years later, Black Elk recalled the scene:

> I did not know then how much was ended that day. But I can see [now] that something else died there in the bloody mud, and was buried in the blizzard. A people's dream died there. It was a beautiful dream.

TAKING ANOTHER LOOK

1. What did Wovoka's vision promise Native Americans?
2. What factors encouraged Native Americans to follow the Ghost Dance?
3. *CRITICAL THINKING* What did Black Elk mean when he said "a people's dream" died at Wounded Knee?

KEY IDEAS

- In 1878, the Northern Cheyenne led by Dull Knife and Little Wolf fled from a reservation in Oklahoma, but were pursued and captured by U.S. troops.

1 The Broken Hoop

- Native Americans on reservations had to depend on government rations because traditional sources of food were no longer available.
- Federal agents tried to end traditional Native American ways of life and force the adoption of new ways, such as farming.

2 Uprooting a Heritage

- Reformers tried to Americanize Native Americans by sending their children to boarding schools.
- In 1887, the Dawes Act divided up reservation lands and resulted in a land-grab in which more than half of all Native American lands were lost.

3 Ghost Dancers

- In the late 1880s, the Ghost Dance, part of a hopeful vision of the future for Native Americans spread quickly among the peoples of the plains.
- Federal officials believed that the Ghost Dances were war dances, and attempted to arrest the leaders.
- In 1890, soldiers surrounded Big Foot's band at Wounded Knee Creek and killed almost 300 Lakota.

WHO, WHAT, WHERE

1. **Who** was Dull Knife?
2. **Where** did the Northern Cheyenne finally settle?
3. **Who** did federal agents hire to bypass the power of Native American chiefs?
4. **What** are sun dances?
5. **Who** were "wards of the nation"?
6. **What** was the Dawes Act?
7. **Who** was Wovoka?
8. **What** was a Ghost Shirt?

9. **Where** did Ghost Dancers flee when troops were sent to the Lakota reservations?

UNDERSTANDING THE CHAPTER

1. Why did Dull Knife and Little Wolf flee from the Northern Cheyenne reservation in Oklahoma?
2. How did federal agents and reformers try to wipe out traditional Native American ways of life?
3. How did the Supreme Court and the Congress act to weaken the Native American nations?
4. How did the U.S. government react to the spread of the Ghost Dance?

MAKING CONNECTIONS

1. What was the connection between the creation of boarding schools for Native American children in the late 1800s and attempts to force Native Americans to abandon their traditional ways of life?
2. What was the connection between life on the reservations and the spread of the Ghost Dance?

WRITING ABOUT HISTORY

1. Imagine you are a Native American coming home from a boarding school. Write four diary entries about the feeling of being in between two worlds.
2. Write an advertisement for "Buffalo Bill" Cody's Wild West Show. Then write a paragraph explaining why you think the show was so popular among white Americans at the same time that Native Americans were being forced to give up their cultures.
3. Imagine you are a Native American leader in 1877. Write a letter to Congress protesting the Dawes Act.
4. Suppose you could interview any one of the Native American leaders discussed in this chapter. Decide who you would interview and write five questions you would like to ask them.

Time Chart

The Time Chart below shows events that were taking place around the world during the years studied in this book.

1600 · 1620 · 1640 · 1660 · 1680 · 1700 · 1720 · 1740

AFRICA, EUROPE, ASIA

1629
The Sefavid Empire in Persia reaches its height.

1639
Foreigners are expelled from Japan.

1644
The Manchu dynasty comes to power in China.

1698
Czar Peter the Great begins the modernization of Russia.

1733
The invention of a weaving machine sets off the Industrial Revolution in Great Britain.

THE AMERICAS

1610
Spanish found Santa Fe in what is now New Mexico.

1619
The first Africans arrive in the English colonies.

1642
Montreal is founded.

1673
Marquette and Joliet explore the Mississippi River.

1717
Spain begins efforts to settle Texas.

THE UNITED STATES

Early 1600s
Native Americans in what is now the U.S. Southwest begin to acquire horses.

1620
Pilgrims found Plymouth Colony.

1647
Massachusetts sets up the first public schools.

Late 1600s
Native Americans from woodlands of the Midwest begin to move to the plains.

1730
Plains Shoshoni acquire horses; Cree and Blackfeet acquire guns.

1600 · 1620 · 1640 · 1660 · 1680 · 1700 · 1720 · 1740

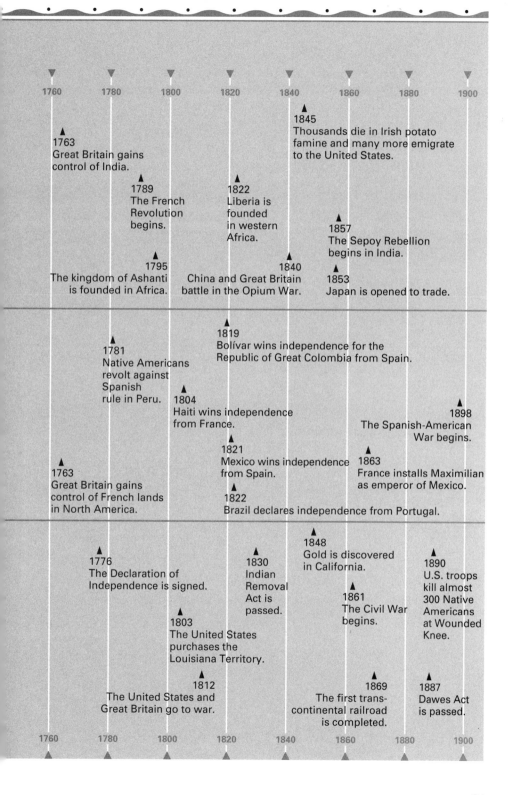

1760 1780 1800 1820 1840 1860 1880 1900

1763
Great Britain gains control of India.

1789
The French Revolution begins.

1822
Liberia is founded in western Africa.

1845
Thousands die in Irish potato famine and many more emigrate to the United States.

1857
The Sepoy Rebellion begins in India.

1795
The kingdom of Ashanti is founded in Africa.

1840
China and Great Britain battle in the Opium War.

1853
Japan is opened to trade.

1819
Bolívar wins independence for the Republic of Great Colombia from Spain.

1781
Native Americans revolt against Spanish rule in Peru.

1804
Haiti wins independence from France.

1898
The Spanish-American War begins.

1821
Mexico wins independence from Spain.

1863
France installs Maximilian as emperor of Mexico.

1763
Great Britain gains control of French lands in North America.

1822
Brazil declares independence from Portugal.

1776
The Declaration of Independence is signed.

1830
Indian Removal Act is passed.

1848
Gold is discovered in California.

1890
U.S. troops kill almost 300 Native Americans at Wounded Knee.

1803
The United States purchases the Louisiana Territory.

1861
The Civil War begins.

1812
The United States and Great Britain go to war.

1869
The first transcontinental railroad is completed.

1887
Dawes Act is passed.

1760 1780 1800 1820 1840 1860 1880 1900

GLOSSARY

The glossary defines important terms used in the book. The page on which a term first appears is given in parentheses at the end of the definition.

Americanize to force members of a minority culture to adopt the ways of the majority of people in the United States (81)

counting coup (koo) Native American practice of proving bravery by touching or striking an enemy in combat (12)

Dawes Act act of Congress passed in 1887 that divided up Native American reservations, also known as the General Allotment Act (83)

Dog Soldiers band of Cheyenne warriors famed for bravery (46)

Ghost Dance religious movement that spread among Native Americans of the plains during the late 1800s; inspired by a vision of a recreation of the earth for Native Americans and the return of ancestors from the dead (85)

literacy rate percentage of people able to read and write (22)

neutrality policy under which a nation does not participate directly or indirectly on either side in a conflict (33)

prairie large area of flat or rolling grasslands, for example, the Great Plains of the United States (6)

ration set amount of goods provided by the government (78)

reservation public land set aside by the government for Native Americans (38)

sun dance religious ceremony held by Native Americans of the plains each fall or spring to ensure earth's continued bounty (79)

travois (trah-VWAH) type of sledge made from a net or platform lashed between two long wooden poles used to carry things and pulled by a dog or a horse (10)

wampum shell beads gathered in strings or belts and used by Native Americans, originally as a record of agreement or treaties and, later, used as money (18)

ward status of being under the care or guidance of another (83)

INDEX

SOURCES

Sources for quotations are given by page number (in parentheses) and in the order in which the quotations appear on each page. **CHAPTER 1** (**4**) Lakota saying, in Leslie Tillet, *Wind on the Buffalo Grass: Native American Artist-Historians* (New York: Da Capo, 1989), p. xiv. (**5**) Black Elk, in John G. Neihardt, *Black Elk Speaks* (Lincoln, NE: University of Nebraska, 1961), p. 7. (**6**) Luther Standing Bear, in T.C. McLuhan, *Touch the Earth: A Portrait of Indian Existence* (New York: Promontory Press, 1971) p. 45. (**10**) Buffalo hunt, in Neihardt, pp. 55-57. (**11**) Pretty Shield, in Frank B. Linderman, *Pretty Shield: Medicine Woman of the Crows* (Lincoln, NE: University of Nebraska, 1932), p. 135. (**12**) Teal Duck, in Thomas E. Mails, *Plains Indians: Dog Soldiers, Bear Men and Buffalo Women* (New York: Promontory Press, 1991), p.28. (**13**) Pretty Shield, in Linderman, p. 134. (**14**) Prayer, in Carolyn Niethammer, *Daughters of the Earth: The Lives and Legends of American Indian Women* (New York: Collier Macmillan, 1977), p.12. (**15**) Brave Buffalo, in McLuhan, p.16; Drinks Water, in Niehardt, p.10. **CHAPTER 2** (**18**) Iroquois, in Ronald Wright, *Stolen Continents: The Americas Through Indian Eyes Since 1492* (New York: Houghton Mifflin, 1992), p. 202. (**20**) Jackson, in Wright, p.214. (**24**) Cherokee constitution, in Wright, p. 224. (**26**) Wilma Mankiller, in Wright, p. 312. **CHAPTER 3** (**30**) Treaty, in Francis P. Prucha, *Great Father: The U.S. Government and the American Indians* (Lincoln, NE: University of Nebraska, 1986), p.139. (**33**) John Ross, in Wright, p. 40; Ross, in Robert M. Utley, *The Indian Frontier of the American West, 1846-1890* (Albuquerque: University of New Mexico, 1984), p. 73. (**34**) Opothle Yahola, in William Katz, *Black Indians: A Hidden Heritage* (New York: Atheneum, 1986), p. 143. (**35**) Seminole chief, in Katz, p. 143. (**37**) John Ross, in Wright, p. 300; Big Eagle, in Alvin M. Josephy, Jr., *The Civil War in the American West* (New York: Knopf, 1991), p. 106. (**38**) Big Eagle, in Josephy, p. 106; Little Crow, Galbraith, and Myrick in Dee Brown, *Bury My Heart at Wounded Knee* (New York: Holt, 1970), p. 40. (**39**) Santee youth, in Brown, p. 43. (**40**) Little Crow, in Josephy, p. 111. (**43**) White Antelope, in Brown, p. 84. **CHAPTER 4** (**46**) Roman Nose, in McLuhan, p. 88; Hancock, in Brown, p. 152. (**47**) Roman Nose and Hancock, in Brown, p. 156. (**48**) "Why do you," in Editors of Time-Life, *The Old West* (New York: Time-Life, 1976), p. 213. (**51**) Sherman, in Ralph K. Andrist, *The Long Death* (New York: Knopf, 1976), p.154. (**52**) Kwahadi chief, in Editors of Time-Life, *The Indians* (New York: Time-Life, 1976), p. 192. (**54**) Old Lady Horse, in Peter Nabokov, editor, *Native American Testimony* (New York: Viking, 1991), p. 175; Satanta, in Andrist, p. 184. (**55**) Satanta, in Brown, p. 248. (**56**) Henson poem, from *Keeper of Arrows: Poems for the Cheyenne* (Milwaukee, WI: Renaissance Books). **CHAPTER 5** (**60**) Pretty Shield, in Linderman, p. 15. (**61**) Pretty Shield, in Linderman, pp. 251-53; Black Elk, in Neihardt, p.8. (**62**) "Land no wider," Neihardt, p. 9. (**63**) Red Cloud, in Utley, p. 213; Fetterman, in Andrist, p. 108. (**65**) Red Cloud, in Time-Life, *The Indians,* p. 200. (**66**) Custer and horse soldier, in Brown, pp. 277, 283. (**67**) Plenty Coups, in Carl Waldman, *Atlas of the North American Indian* (New York: Facts on File, 1985), p. 153; Sitting Bull, in Time-Life, *The Old West*, p. 237. (**69**) Boys, in Neihardt, p.109; White Bull, in Tillet, p. 99. (**71**) Pretty Shield, in Linderman, p. 251. (**72**) Joseph, in Time-Life, The Indians, p. 193. (**73**) Joseph, in David Lavender, *Let Me Be Free* (New York: HarperCollins, 1992), p. 321. **CHAPTER 6** (**76**) Little Wolf, in McLuhan, p. 145. (**78**) Sweezy, in Nabokov, p. 211. (**79**) Pretty Shield, in Linderman, p. 251. (**80**) Blackfeet, in Nabokov, p. 225; Black Elk, in Neihardt, p. 218. (**81**) Sitting Bull, in Brown, p. 427; Black Elk, in Neihardt, p. 196. (**82**) Cherokee leader, in Nabokov, p. 215; Carlisle founder, in Utley, p. 219. (**83**) Sweezy, in Nabokov, p.208; teacher, in Utley, p. 219. (**84**) Wovoka, in Richard Jensen, R. Eli Paul, and John Carter, *Eyewitness at Wounded Knee* (Lincoln, NE: University of Nebraska, 1991), p.6. (**85**) Wovoka, in Jensen et al., p. 12. (**87**) Weasel Bear, in Brown, p. 444; Black Elk, in Neihardt, p. 270.